PRAISE FOR

"The Tuning In series truly embodies the excellence that this award was created to celebrate."
–National Indie Excellence Awards

"A very enjoyable, thought-provoking read with a sprinkle of action, a little helping of romance, and a good chunk of suspense."
–Readers' Favorite Official Review

"A commendable series with surprising moments of profundity."
–Kirkus Reviews

"Bravo! Love the premise! An especially fine work of magical realism."
–Amazon Kindle Scout Editorial Team

Winner: Science Fiction
–American Fiction Awards

Finalist,Thriller & Suspense
–Forward Reviews

TUNING

IN

BOOK ONE OF THE
TUNING IN SERIES

A NOVEL BY

RICHARD ROBERTS

TUNING IN
Published by Highcrest Books
San Anselmo, CA

ISBN (Paperback Edition): 978-1-948681-00-1

For Lily and Charlie

Tuesday, October 2

Jon Gunnarson felt the energy rise within his opponent an instant before she attacked. Then she charged forward, hands and feet slashing in complex patterns, faster than he could think and react to.

But he'd become one with her and the space around them and somehow his body knew exactly where to be. In a fluid, weightless dance, he twisted her wrist and used her momentum to bring her safely past him and down.

In that brief respite, an ethereal, feminine voice filled his mind. "This is not Jon."

He'd never heard it before, but knew it meant that his movements were coming from somewhere, from something other than himself. Distracted, his deep connection to his opponent Chodak Neema and the space around them faltered. He saw again the crowd of people lining the walls of the dojo, the hint of concern rising on his sensei's face.

Neema rose up from her fall.

Jon backed away to buy himself a few seconds and considered asking for a short break to reconnect. After all, he was hoping to earn rokudan, the highest level in the martial art aikido. But to him, the message felt belittling, denying him any credit in one of his finest moments.

So he resisted, wanting to prove he could win without relying on his *gift*. His ego took control and he watched for clues of her next attack.

Neema's knuckles suddenly banged into his face and the side of his head, like ball point hammers.

He reeled backward, blinking, and noticed how she was turning again, trying to get behind him. He thought to follow her, to grab her wrist and pull her arm.

Neema reversed, as though she'd felt his intent, and slammed her elbow into his temple.

An explosion of sound and light filled his mind. He lost control of his body and the gray vinyl mat rushed up to meet him.

It took him a long moment to accept what had happened. Then he slammed his fist down, the floor booming with his failure.

Minutes later, Jon paced outside the dojo, scrubbing his face with his towel. He realized what a stupid risk he'd taken trying to think his way through a fight.

The large door of the converted California barn squeaked open. Neema snuck out and came to him, flapping in her sandals, wrapped in her maroon robe. She kept her eyes low and opened her hand to the wooden bench. "What happened?" she said, once they'd settled next to each other.

"I don't know," he said, not ready to admit the strange voice he'd heard.

The large wind chime gonged, low and heavy in the warm breeze.

"When I learned who I'd fight today, who you were," she said. "I thought how this was life coming full-circle." Wrinkles framed her narrow, dark eyes. Patches of gray and white mixed together in the stubble on her scalp.

"Yeah, quite the coincidence. I was afraid I might hurt you." Jon had been seven, visiting the Tiger's Nest monastery in Bhutan with his mother, when he first met Neema. She'd introduced him to aikido, a martial art focused on bringing both fighters to a safe place. They hadn't spoken again until today, thirty-two years later, when she visited his dojo while traveling in her duties as a Buddhist nun.

"I think if I'd won today," he said, "Sensei Haruto would have advanced me to rokudan."

"You try again."

"Today wasn't just about rank. He's hiring an instructor, a protégé. If Jordan rises to rokudan first, he'll probably get the job."

A thump came from the barn as someone tumbled to the mat inside.

Jon didn't want to face his sensei and Jordan as they came out. He led Neema up a steep deer trail to an outcropping of rock above the dojo. Tan hills rolled in every direction, dotted with the black cows of West Marin dairy farms. Leaning on the rock, he had a clear view of the dojo, of Jordan's family hugging him on the front porch. This place, Jon's main source of social interaction for the past two years, now felt almost foreign.

"It's beautiful here," Neema said.

"It is. I live right over that hill. A town called Woodacre." His tiny cottage came to mind, silent and empty on the shady side of the valley. As much as he wanted to get away from the dojo, he also dreaded going home alone.

Jon's sensei came out of the barn and said something to Jordan. The group burst into cheers, followed by more hugs.

"Jordan's a rokudan," Jon said. "I didn't get the job."

They were silent for a few moments, the sun hot and bright.

"I remember our first aikido lesson at Tiger's Nest," Neema said. "You joining with me right away. And your bond with your mother."

Jon's unique brain structure had given him a simple form of telepathy with his mom.

"I don't know if you heard but she died of a brain tumor a few months after we got home."

"No, I didn't know. I'm so sorry."

"So I don't do that anymore. But when I interact with someone, or even think about them, I feel what they're feeling. And it's getting worse."

Neema narrowed her eyes.

"I'm what people call an empath. An extreme one. It's like I have no personal boundary. Like I'm wide open."

"Ahh. This is what makes you a great sensei."

"It helps me get into the zone, for sure. But when I'm with other people out in the world, I lose myself. I can't resist what's coming in. I have to pull away."

"I sensed that in our fight. You were deeply connected until, you weren't."

"Well, that was something new." Jon took a breath. "I heard this weird voice in my head. It said, 'This is not Jon.' Like it wasn't me directing my body, it was my condition. And, I don't know, it made me want to win by myself."

"Your self?" She looked down to the barn. "True victory is victory over oneself," she said, reciting the Japanese characters carved above the dojo's entrance.

Jon knew that *oneself* here referred to the ego, the sense of "I," the everyday brain that thinks and plans. He knew his ego had cost him the fight and the job he wanted. "Do you have any idea what that voice was?" he said.

"The quieter you become, the more you're able to hear," she said, quoting Rumi.

Jon opened his hands and shook his head.

"I'll sit with this," she said.

"Thanks. What I really need help with is controlling this empath thing. I've read the books, the Internet, even meds. I need more of a boundary so I don't have to be alone so much. Can you help me?"

"Perhaps." Neema held his gaze.

A warmth spread across his chest.

"But," she said, "My American tour is finished. I fly home tonight to get ready for my annual visit to Tiger's Nest."

Her mentioning again the place of his happy memories with his mom, the place he'd thought magical as a boy, flooded him with nostalgia. As if regressing to that state of mind, an immature plan took hold. He could meet Neema there again. She'd help him go deep within himself and manage his condition.

His phone dinged in his backpack with a reminder.

"Neema, I have to go now. But I'd love to visit you in Bhutan."

"Oh, I don't know. Write me a letter and we'll see. Haruto can give you the address."

Jon held her hand as they ventured back down the steep path. They bowed low as they said goodbye. And as he pedaled his mountain bike up the steep climb back into town, his mind raced with vague notions of camping out near the monastery and living like a Buddhist pilgrim.

Ten minutes later, he crested the hill and took a moment to catch his breath. The sight of the yoga studio resting on the valley floor below shifted his thoughts from Tiger's Nest to Danielle Murphy.

He lowered his bike seat and sped down the steep trail. Before he could book his trip to Bhutan, he had to endure his most difficult client.

###

Ella Sandström slid the glass door shut. "We can talk out here for a minute."

Her new research assistant, Oliver Mabry, sat opposite her on the deck of her hotel room in Bhutan.

"How was your flight?" She asked. He'd just made the nineteen-hour journey from London.

He yawned and checked his phone. "Okay, at least I'm getting iMessages on the Wi-Fi."

"Yes, you can get texts here, but you need to use the hotel phones to make calls." She unconsciously patted her jeans pocket and then remembered she'd left her phone muted on her desk during the experiment.

Oliver held his phone up to the glass door, took a picture of the monks inside, and then tapped out a text.

Patience, Ella told herself, sitting in one of the low deck chairs. She knew that every detail of Oliver's experience here would make it back to his father, Wendell Mabry, Ella's department head at the University of Oxford, in England. Wendell had suggested she take on his seventeen-year-old son during his extended autumn break. "A free set of hands," he'd said.

And Ella couldn't refuse her boss.

Oliver "How can they just sit like that?" he said, jerking his thumb toward the monks inside.

Ella took a conscious breath, forced a smile, and looked past him at strands of mist weaving between the cliffs on the far side of the valley.

"They sit still to see the mind from the inside," she said. "I look at the brain from the outside, but we're after the same thing. And we usually agree."

Ella's schooling and career in science had taught her to deny subjectivity and intuition. Now she sought to answer the hardest question in neuroscience: to understand the material basis in the brain of consciousness and human connection.

"So, Oliver, what do you know about social neuroscience?"

"Oh, not much. Don't see dad very often."

Because he never leaves the bloody campus, Ella wanted to say. "That's okay. Social neuroscience is about the brain's role in people's interactions and morality. My work here focuses on empathy and feeling connected to others."

Oliver glanced down to his phone; he couldn't seem to look her in the eye.

This, Ella thought, was going to be a long ten days. "A year ago," she said, "I started an experiment, my pet project as your father calls it, with twenty monks at a nearby monastery. I asked them to spend a part of their daily meditation focusing on sending and receiving feelings of surrender, oneness, or compassion to each other. They took turns and then asked each other afterward if they'd perceived the correct feeling. They didn't need to keep track; it was simply a practice."

"That's cool. Uh, so, what am I going to be doing here?"

Ella looked again to the cliffs to buy herself a moment, wondering again how she could possibly put Oliver to use. "Well, two things. First, we'll use EEG to measure the monks' brainwave frequencies. We want to see which areas of their brains light up when they attempt to send these feelings to each other. And then we'll use the MRI truck down in the parking lot to measure how their brains have changed over the past year."

"How their brains changed?"

"Yes, it's surprisingly easy to influence neural network patterns."

"Wow, so you're like, watching their brains change in there?"

Ella wished she'd told her boss Wendell to bugger off. "Not in real time. It usually takes about three months to see any change. We're using the EEG to see which areas of their brains are activating."

Oliver nodded slowly.

Ella wasn't sure if he'd really understood but at this point, she couldn't stay away from her monitors any longer. She'd started recording the first send/receive session right after Oliver had arrived, and now she had to see what was happening. "Hang on a moment, will you? Be right back."

Inside, two monks in saffron robes sat back-to-back in silence, white EEG sensor caps covering their shaved heads. Ella crept to her monitors, careful not to catch her foot on the thick cords from the machines.

Her phone lay face up on her desk. She noticed three texts from her daughter, Jady.

"Are you coming home this weekend?"

"Guess you're busy."

"Never mind, I have plans anyway."

Ella knew she should call Jady back right away—they hadn't spoken in days—but the first results of her study were right in front of her. She had to take a peek. She flicked her mouse, allowing colored, 3-D simulations of the two monks' brains to fill her screens.

"Yes," Ella whispered. And then to herself, *yes, yes, yes.* She was experiencing one of those moments when everything clicked, when a lifetime of sacrifice and effort seemed worth it.

She opened another window and lost herself in the data.

###

Jon maneuvered his bike through the back door of the yoga studio and into the employee common area.

His client Danielle, a striking and recently divorced woman in her mid-forties, sat reclined with her phone on the shabby Ikea sofa. Her pink sundress came mid-thigh and her toned legs crossed at the knees.

He nodded *hello* with a tight-lipped smile.

He felt her study him as he leaned his bike against the stale mound of unclaimed mats. His thin t-shirt and running shorts suddenly felt obscenely snug on him and he wished he'd stopped by his cottage to change.

A yoga teacher's voice, amplified to carry over a Van Morrison tune, called out directions to the hatha flow class in the front room.

"Tree pose. Try closing your eyes," the voice instructed. "Don't be afraid to fall out. Let your ego go."

Jon no longer taught yoga classes. The varied jumble of feelings he took in from a group had become overwhelming. His private yoga sessions had evolved over the years from instruction to silent eye-gazing sessions where he not only shared his clients' emotions but absorbed their negative feelings. He healed his clients like a sponge.

As he unlocked the door to the room he shared with Jill, the studio's masseuse, Danielle came close behind him, her heady energy reminding him of their previous sessions, each more uncomfortable than the last. Reminding him to resist.

The small room felt like a sauna. Jill had left her space heater on and the shades open to the glaring parking lot. The scent of coconut massage oil filled the space with a tropical, sultry haze.

As if every second counted, he peeled off his backpack, pulled out his phone, and set the timer for an hour. He slid the massage table against the window to make room and was about to close the curtains when he stopped, hoping that leaving them open would inhibit Danielle's antics.

They positioned the two office chairs facing each other. She slid hers closer than usual and they sat. The brown vinyl seat pads hissed. His right knee came between hers.

Jon began staring into her hazel eyes. He shifted his gaze from one to the other and then focused on her dilated left pupil—like a tiny black tunnel into her mind. He could still see her full head: the fine lines at the corners of her eyes, her light brown hair, her pink lips, and the freckles dotting her sun-browned cheeks and nose.

A car door thudded shut outside, followed by the beep of the alarm activating.

His head ached from where Neema had hit him.

Keeping his gaze locked on her left pupil, he deepened his breath, went inward, and felt his connection with her and the space around them take hold.

Soon he felt a tightness building in his temples and realized he was clenching his jaw. A few moments later, he felt fiercely angry, his mind buzzing. He'd tried to resist, but her anger was now his.

As usual, he had no control over the process. He felt the physical sensation of his clients' emotions in his body, and then he understood their situation.

Danielle blinked away tears, making dark spots on her sundress as they fell. It seemed as if she were looking at him not merely to see him, but to reveal something about herself. That underneath her flirty shell, there burned a red-hot stove.

He cried with her, somehow knowing that her rage involved her ex-husband's infidelity.

After sitting in a semi-hypnotic state for about twenty minutes, he felt the rage coming from her subside, as if she'd been drained of poison for a time. Her shift happened much sooner than in their previous sessions, but Jon knew that what he'd absorbed from her would still stay with him for hours.

With new focus, her eyes flitted over his mouth, his ears, his hair, and his forehead, pausing with a look of concern at the swelling on his temple. Then, seemingly satisfied with her preliminary inspection, she met his stare, tilted her head, and sighed.

Game on, Jon thought.

As if he'd said those words out loud, she tilted her head to the other side, this time blinking, adding dimples and suppressing a laugh. Like a spouse sharing an inside joke. She couldn't seem to stop smiling now, giddy to be there.

This was a dangerous game. But after his complete failure at the dojo, it felt good to be wanted. He told himself he could handle it. He'd never let anything happen. He just had to restrain himself for another half-hour.

Danielle's counter stare resumed and she seemed to be settling down until a long, muffled chant, *Oooomm*, came from the front studio. As if reawakened, her eyes started wandering again. They shifted down to his mouth, then to his chest.

He had the fleeting, silly concern she could see his heart pounding through his thin t-shirt. Jon fought to keep his face neutral. He still carried her anger even as he resisted his body's reactions to her new mood.

Her lips parted. In the silence he heard her quick breaths. As she became more aroused, Jon couldn't help feeling the same, creating a feedback loop of desire.

She dropped her focus lower, to his lap, and stayed there.

As though Danielle had some kind of perverted superpower, his shorts grew painfully tight.

Finally, she crept her eyes back up to meet his. She grinned.

Jon licked his lips, and then wondered why on earth he'd done such a thing.

Her eyes widened, and she bit her lower lip, holding her teeth there.

Jon did his best to separate himself from the situation. He never dated clients and figured that she only wanted him because he wasn't attainable. That she believed if she got him to break his code as a healer, it would prove her worth, prove she was so desirable that he'd risk his career for her.

Her lip turned white where her teeth gripped it. It looked painful.

He felt her desire, so he knew she wasn't acting. And from his psychology education, it didn't seem like she was transferring an unresolved need onto him. Even though they'd only ever spoken a few sentences, this lust felt directed squarely at him.

She released her lip, swollen and red.

Thirty more minutes of this?

The small room felt even warmer now, and stuffy with musky sweat, like a hot yoga class. Jon blinked perspiration from his eyes and glanced away, for a moment of relief, something he never did in these sessions. By separating his gaze, he became more aware of the heavy ache in his shorts. Shifting his hips to adjust himself, his right knee brushed the inside of her thigh.

She shivered, sucked in a breath and then pounced, grabbing his head and kissing him with frantic, teeth-bumping intensity.

He rose, afraid they might topple backward. Danielle's legs wrapped tightly around him but he didn't stop her, or himself, because after his humiliating failure at the dojo, he craved any kind of connection.

"The table," she said between pants.

Jon placed her on the massage table and allowed Danielle to pull his body on top of her.

She peeled off his running shorts using her hands and feet as they kissed.

Out of the corner of his eye, Jon caught movement outside in the parking lot and turned to find a cluster of women, who'd just left the studio, staring at them. He reached up, and exposing himself fully, tugged the curtains shut.

Danielle guided him onto his back and then straddled him, kneeling upright, hands on her chest, eyes closed. Lost in her own world, requiring only one part of him to serve her need.

And after, she dressed and left. Neither having spoken a word.

Jon sat cross-legged on the table. He brushed his arms, legs and chest with his hands, a technique that had helped him in the past clear other people's feelings from his psyche. Even as he did, he knew that all he'd taken in would stay with him until he spent hours running, practicing yoga or sitting on his porch. Because lately his connections had been deeper and the strain of resisting his clients' emotions more difficult.

A car door shut outside his window. He cracked open the curtain to see Danielle adjusting her hair in her rear-view mirror.

Layered beneath the anger and the lust he'd absorbed from her, he felt both hollow and heavy at the same time. These feelings, he knew, were his own.

She must have seen the curtains moving, because before she backed out, she glanced to him with a satisfied smirk.

His phone's timer jolted him, chiming from the floor.

Bhutan, he thought. He would visit Neema in Bhutan.

# # #

Jeffrey Venn brought his palms together in front of his heart.

He'd recently seen George Clooney do this in a movie and liked how thoughtful it made him look. Plus, he found that copying

Clooney's mannerisms reinforced his uncanny likeness to the famous actor. Which never hurt.

He sat safe behind his immaculate glass desk in his bright, Times Square corner office. His Marketing Director, Lex Moller, sat across from him. He tore his gaze away from her and turned to smile at the video-conference monitor at the end of his desk.

"Max, I've still got it. We're going to make a killing. Our big bet this year is meditation tech."

Most people knew Jeffrey as the CEO of Venn Digital, a large Internet Marketing agency in Manhattan. Few knew of his fraudulent and wildly profitable division called Person8. The division's mantra, Money for Nothing, had inspired gray hat schemes such as locking teens into ringtone subscriptions and black hat scams like stealing college students' money with the promise of employment in non-existent companies.

Venn tapped a key and his video conference screen filled with the words, *TUNING IN* and the image of a beautiful young couple wearing headphones.

"Tuning In, a mobile meditation app," Venn said.

"You're too late," the voice on the speaker said. "That market's saturated."

Max Harding, the gravelly voice on the phone and Person8's sole outside investor, had known Venn long enough to interrupt.

"Hold on, I've got a twist. Tuning In makes you telepathic."

The voice on the speaker cackled.

Venn turned down the volume and waited for the laughter—which had become a coughing fit—to subside.

"Sentiment analysis shows strong interest in telepathy among certain segments," Venn said. "You see the *New York Times* article I sent you, about that autistic kid? I helped get that story picked up."

A week earlier, an autistic girl in Los Angeles had demonstrated simple telepathy with her mother: correctly identifying numbers on cards that her mother viewed while behind a screen. Scientists at USC had conducted the tests under controlled conditions. *Nature* had published the findings.

As a test, Venn's Person8 contractors in Eastern Europe had posted a video of the girl across hundreds of fake social media accounts. When it had gone viral, Venn decided to double his investment in the Tuning In app and personally supervise the project.

"I'm recording that kid's brainwaves to use in the app," Venn said.

"You signed her?"

"Not yet. The mother's playing hard ball. All of a sudden, she's worried about her kid."

Venn checked the small video image of himself in the lower corner to make sure he looked confident.

"It's fine if I can't make a deal. I've got a top psychic ready to go."

Harding grunted. "You said you're gonna use brainwaves in the app?"

"It's called brainwave entrainment. It's an audio track that puts your brain in different states, like more alert or more relaxed. That kind of thing. Been around for years. There's an attachment that describes it."

The sound of papers rustling carried over the speaker. Harding liked to print things out.

Venn rose and paced behind his desk; he moved through the world like a lifelong run-on sentence: one gesture or movement continually shifting into the next, never the sense of *I'm there*. He let out a breath.

"Let's keep moving, okay?" Tapping a key, he brought a slide of charts onto the screen. "Market sizing and competitive gap analysis..."

Twenty slides later, Venn was feeling good about how the presentation was going. He clicked on the final slide titled Your Investment and put it on the line.

"We're going big on this one, Max. We each put in three hundred grand for media. I'll make it as real as I can and then blow it out."

"Make it real? A telepathy app?"

"Remember, I'm shooting videos on location, hiring real people to produce this. The spiritual soccer moms will eat it up," Venn said, as though he'd ever actually known a spiritual soccer mom. "It's hot right now and there's no other player in this space. We'll have a solid six-month run."

Venn gave his best sideways grin.

"Alright, alright. I'm in," Harding said, his watery eyes staring out of the screen. "You think you're gonna have time for this? With the investigation?"

Lex looked up from her laptop, scowling, as though Max had personally attacked her boss.

"No problem at all," Venn said. "We gave them a mountain of files and I have an interview in three weeks to discuss it."

Harding made a grunting sound. "Well, keep me in the loop on that."

Venn agreed and then ended the conference.

Lex was already up and heading for the office door. She'd worn her short leather skirt today, as though in honor of the big pitch. Venn sprang from his chair and moved to catch her.

"We got it, babe."

"Good thing, 'cause we're flying out in a week," she said over her shoulder.

Venn put his arm across her chest as he came up from behind her.

"We're gonna be in the mountains," he said, speaking softly into her ear. "Get yourself some hot hiking outfits."

She spun out of his arm and faced him. "Yeah, like that video game chick."

"Lara Croft, Tomb Raider. Perfect."

She shook her head a fraction and gave him one of those smiles he wasn't sure how to read.

"Jeffrey, do you—?" She stopped herself.

"Do I what?"

"Never mind. I'll get you some gear too."

She smiled again, her eyes as flat as ever, and Venn wondered what went on in that sexy little head of hers.

###

Jon sunk into his couch, phone in hand, ready to book his trip to Bhutan. Twenty minutes later, he knew it wasn't happening. There was no way he could afford it—he earned just enough to cover his expenses. Plus, all visitors to the country were required to have a visa.

His chance to earn more had been to become an aikido instructor. But he'd lost that chance when he'd tried to think his way through the fight. The loud voice filled his mind and spoke directly to him. So different from the random words and phrases he heard sometimes before sleep.

Neema had said she'd meditate about it, but she'd left the country. She didn't have a phone or email, so Jon wasn't sure if he'd ever speak to her again. He realized he'd have to figure this out on his own. He opened the browser on his phone and searched "hearing voices".

His first surprise was learning that up to a quarter of the general population heard thought-like voices and that most of these voice-hearers had no psychotic disorder. This meant that millions of sane people heard some kind of voices in their heads.

Posts on various forums claimed these voices were a form of telepathy. Some cited studies proving a slight telepathic ability in humans.

The strange voice he'd heard in the fight didn't feel like telepathy. What he heard from his mother had never manifested itself as a clear voice; it had come to him as a knowing.

No, what he heard earlier that day seemed more like the accounts he'd read about from countless people throughout history, from Socrates to Gandhi: that he'd heard the voice of the divine.

But what kind of message was "This is not Jon" for the divine to give? Why point out that it wasn't really him doing the fighting? It didn't feel like something the universe would say. It felt more like the teasing he'd had as a kid growing up in Iceland, where everyone in his tiny town rolled their eyes at him and his parents for being *so sensitive*.

Maybe, he thought, since his parents were both empaths and most of his relatives were awkward loners, there was a hereditary, biological basis for this new voice. Something in his brain.

He refined his Google search and found a video of scientists at University College London using fMRIs to detect the neural activity of people while they were hearing voices. The image displayed a lanky, balding man and a pale, intense-looking woman with short, light brown hair pointing to colored brain maps. In the video, the woman did most of the talking.

Jon watched the video repeatedly to try and keep up with her commentary, but he wasn't really listening to what she was saying.

She had captivated him. He studied her every move, how she brought her hand to her ear to pull back locks of hair that weren't there. Had she recently cut it? Jon wondered. Just as he thought this, she started to smile.

He froze the video, took a screenshot, and then tossed his phone onto the couch. In the gloom of his living room, he blinked away the screen's glare.

The cottage ticked as it cooled.

He pictured himself slumped on the sofa, taking screenshots of random women on the Internet. An odd hermit. All at once, he wanted to scream, to throw his phone through the window, but he held himself back, realizing that his anger was likely due to the aftereffects of his session with Danielle. Her feelings still burned in him like the white afterimage of his phone did now on his eyes.

Time to sit, he decided.

Jon liked to sit on his porch. He didn't think of it as meditating. There were no mantras or special techniques. He just sat silently, sometimes with his eyes open, sometimes closed, as if he were waiting for someone or something to arrive. With no friends, no pets, no TV, no computer or hobbies outside of running, yoga, and aikido, Jon sat for between six and eight hours a day.

He rose, and before going to the porch, headed to the kitchen to make a cup of tea. Oddly enough, Jon had an innate map of the more solid patches of his hardwood floor and even at six-two and one hundred and ninety pounds, he could, by uneven slides and long steps, navigate from the couch to the fridge without his tiny cottage sounding like an old ship in a storm. As if he wasn't even there.

He wiped the stove with a dishtowel and deliberated which tea felt right for a night like this. A few minutes later, clutching a mug of smelly valerian root tea, he eased into his old wicker chair out front, awed by the gathering of stars.

The smoke alarm wailed.

He scrambled back inside to find the towel flaming on the stove.

He'd left the electric burner on.

Using bacon tongs to snatch up the towel, he doused it in the sink, coughing from the black smoke. With his eyes squinting and his shoulders at his ears, he twisted the alarm from the ceiling and yanked out the rectangular battery.

Bella, his neighbor's insane terrier, was barking nonstop.

Cleaning up the ashes with his last surviving dish towel (this wasn't his first fire), he asked himself why he did this, what his passive aggressive subconscious was trying to tell him. He could make himself crazy with his psychology degree.

Bella was dragged inside, and silence returned. But tonight, sitting on the porch, sipping his tea, the quiet just felt empty. A wave of exhaustion washed over him, and he walked straight to his bedroom, ignoring the creaking floor, and lay on his bed, ready to be entertained and amazed by his new nightly pastime. He breathed deeply, let his mind open, and quickly reached the twilight between waking and sleep.

And then he listened.

Words and phrases, random statements, each with a different voice, began softly popping in and out of his mind every few minutes: "We're going there tomorrow." "Alphabet." "Organic coffee." "Made from balsa wood."

The statements were clear and distinct but completely unexplainable—he'd kept track of them before and they bore no relation to events in his life. And, unlike what he'd heard in the fight, they didn't seem directed to him. They felt more like he was catching snippets of many different conversations.

He thought of the people he'd read about on the Internet—the ones who heard voices, too. Did they hear things like this? Had his voices always been there unnoticed in his mind or were they getting louder lately? One question haunted him more than he wanted to admit. Was he going crazy?

He warned himself that after losing the aikido instructor job and then his misconduct with a client, the last thing he needed to do was to waste his time listening to gibberish that popped into his head. It wasn't conventional behavior. His college professor had said the task of a psychologist was to shift their patient to a conventional reality. Jon thought how none of his therapists or their meds had been able to do that for him.

He tossed and turned, thinking that his abnormal bedtime ritual could be making him worse. Maybe this was why he heard that voice in the fight. The voice that had made him lose. He had to stop this nonsense and, like it or not, give up trying to disconnect. Yes, he was hypersensitive, but he also had to pay his rent, so tomorrow he had to schedule some clients.

Wednesday, October 3

Jon woke before sunrise to the sound of howling coyotes. He pushed himself out of his warm bed, pulled on his running gear, and chugged some water. He went out the back door and, shivering, pulled the hose across the cracked earth to fill bowls for any thirsty deer who lived in the open space behind his cottage.

Then off he set, flopping his heavy feet in front of him up the steep fire road, birds gossiping as he passed. His neck and shoulders screamed for him to stop, reminding him of his face plant on the mat the day before. He pushed through the agony and reached the ridgeline to see the low, glaring sun catch the windows of the San Francisco towers in the distance.

He passed by a young family coming the other way, friendly neighbors also up early. Tiny hands popped out of a Baby Bjorn, gripping daddy's thumbs.

Jon thought to smile, but after they'd passed, he realized he probably hadn't. A familiar ache rose in his chest, and then up into his throat. He asked himself why he couldn't have little fingers holding him that way.

Always ready for questions like that, his mind took him back thirty years, to sitting in his father's dented pickup in the graveyard of his hometown of Hofn, a small fishing village on the East coast of Iceland. Lights and bonfires spread across the town, celebrating the Twelfth Night of Christmas, but that year Jon hadn't dressed up as an elf, nor his parents as Vikings. There were no songs, fireworks or plastic jugs of Malt and Appelsin to drink.

Fifteen feet of icy, packed snow covered the gravestones and landmarks, but young Jon had imagined that somehow, on that icy white expanse, his father had skidded to a stop directly above his mother's grave. At the time, he'd hoped his dad had brought them to this place on this night to talk about their sadness and to start recovering, rebuilding their lives.

The stench of rank fish and cigarette smoke filled the truck. Gunnar, his father, sucked at his silver flask, scratched his gray beard, and then belched.

Jon had felt a wave of nausea.

A moment later, Gunnar grunted and fumbled for the door handle, which was stuck as usual. Unable to open it in time, his father gushed vomit onto the steering wheel and the dashboard.

Gunnar must have felt better because despite the foul, tangy odor filling the cab, Jon's nausea eased, allowing the familiar, heavy sadness to dominate.

After a time, Gunnar said, "You've got to be careful, Jon."

He stole a glance over to his father who, by the light of the full moon and white snow, was gripping the wheel, his eyes shut.

"Our kind," Gunnar said, referring to their little family of extreme empaths, "We can love. We can be close to people, but we shouldn't. It's too much for us."

Now, the rising California sun in his watering eyes, Jon remembered what he'd learned on that night: that loving someone would end up hurting him so badly it would ruin his life. That he couldn't have a wife, or tiny hands to hold his thumbs because the price of love for someone like him was too high.

Six miles later, and bounding along the ridge, Jon's runner's high finally kicked in, making him feel as though he could run forever. His stride came quick and loose, his mind as open as the pale morning sky. He knew every rock on the path, every leaf in the trees.

Bliss.

Maybe he needed to accept what he was, he reasoned, accept the life he had.

Showered, his head clear, comfortable in his usual faded jeans and t-shirt, Jon settled in his favorite chair on the front porch to review his daunting list of appointment requests. The first, most recent one came from Danielle, with the title, “I NEED another session.”

Suddenly feeling very heavy, as if he might crush his old wicker chair, he lifted his gaze across the valley, to the familiar patterns of green oaks, dark against the tan grass, and a pair of turkey vultures circling in the distance. He’d been focusing on trying to understand the voice he heard during the fight and on facing up to the consequences of his loss. Now, in the morning sun, in his favorite place to sit, what he’d done with Danielle hit him hard.

He stood, started pacing the porch, and asked himself how he could have done something so wrong. How he could have been so weak.

She’d started it, he tried telling himself. He didn’t encourage it.

Are you sure about that? he answered back. You didn’t stop it. You should have dropped her as a client weeks ago.

I was managing it, he said to himself.

You were fantasizing about her after every session.

Okay, yes, I wanted her, and I liked the attention, but…

You got too deep with someone, which itself isn’t okay, his voice of reason countered. And, worse, she’s a client.

She jumped on *me* and clearly, she was totally fine with it.

You can’t go back to Woodacre Yoga. You abused the power dynamic because you’re lonely and desperate for any kind of connection.

I can’t have normal connections, Jon argued with himself.

And you can’t trust yourself with clients anymore.

Jon shook his head. He knew his inner critic was right.

Frustrated, he kicked his old wicker chair against the house, snapping two of its legs and badly stubbing his toe in the process.

He hobbled to sit on his porch steps.

The vultures across the valley had tightened their circle. They lowered, and with their broad black wings flapping, disappeared into a gully.

Rubbing his aching toe, Jon imagined what poor critter lay before them.

His career as a healer was over, he realized, which was just as well since it was getting way too hard anyway.

He pulled out his phone and drafted an email first to Amy, the owner of Woodacre Yoga and then to his entire client base, informing them of his decision. As his finger hovered over the Send command, the full reality of his situation sunk in.

He could no longer earn a living using the only two skills he had, aikido and healing. Not only that, he was losing his only two communities. He envisioned himself becoming even more of a hermit, cycling between miserable, menial jobs for the rest of his life.

But he had to do this.

He pressed Send.

The valley looked the same. His toe still hurt. He took off his sneaker to examine the wound. Thankfully, nothing seemed broken.

While sitting there, his mind went back to his lifelong question of how to block other people's emotions. He'd tried so many techniques, to no avail.

After a few minutes of feeling sorry for himself, he pulled up a psychics' forum website, hoping to find some new advice. The most active string was about communicating with cats. With nothing better to do, he tapped on a link titled "Opportunities" and found a long list of posts, mostly psychics offering readings or requests for psychics to submit their credentials for retreats. He briefly considered listing himself there, but his stomach clenched, and he kept scrolling.

A month-old post caught his eye, titled, "Help develop a new meditation app." The post read, "Travel to Bhutan, high in the Himalayas between the Tibetan Plateau and India, where ancient Buddhist traditions remain vibrant, unaffected by modern life..." He'd stopped breathing at the word Bhutan, so he took a breath and finished reading.

Thumbs zipping across the screen, he responded to the ad while smiling and thanking the universe. Jon accepted the synchronicity of finding exactly what he needed. He paid close attention and knew things like this happened all the time. Sometimes he wondered if he saw patterns and signs that weren't really there. But this time he couldn't deny the clear link between what he'd thought and what had manifested around him.

The company's reply came quickly, an email saying he was too late, the decision had been made and the person they'd selected was set to fly out in a week.

Really?

It had all seemed so right.

Jon went inside and flopped on his bed. He turned on his side to see the familiar bright, hopeful smiles of him as a boy and his mom, holding hands on a steep trail, the Tiger's Nest monastery in the distance behind them. The only framed photo he had.

How had he not mentioned this in his first response?

Jon took a picture of the photo and emailed it to the company, adding a link to his ninety-six glowing Yelp reviews.

They got back to him within the hour requesting a phone interview.

Jon whooped, leapt out of bed, and paced his creaky cottage, sure he'd be chosen as a second candidate. He was already imagining his meeting with Neema at Tiger's Nest.

After a few minutes, he settled back on his porch steps where it occurred to him how tough the long journey would be. Not only would he be sharing other travelers' feelings, but he'd have to tolerate his extreme sensitivity to a range of foul smells, temperature swings, loud noises and the blinding light of the plane windows. Then, once he'd made it there, he'd have to work closely with strangers on the app project.

It wasn't going to be easy, but of course he had to go, because if anyone could help him, it was Neema.

Monday, October 15

(Twelve Days Later)

Ella arranged her last set of colored brain maps on her bed, having run out of room on her walls. Stepping back, she thought how it looked like a creepy paper quilt.

The results she'd seen during the first recording ten days earlier had held up, and she called her assistant Oliver into her bedroom to share the news.

"Look at these." Ella pointed to color-coded numbers on each sheet. "Whenever our monks focused on thinking or receiving messages of surrender, oneness or compassion, their brain states cluster around three specific frequencies in the gamma brain wave range. Here, on our last batch of MRI's, the pattern's clear. Look at the Right Temporal-Parietal Junctions. They've grown a lot since last year and the activity level there for all of them is maxed."

"The TPJ's for hearing voices, right?" Oliver said.

"No, but it's related. Where did you read that?"

"On your Wikipedia page."

"Oh. Yes, about ten years ago, we researched treatment options for Audio Verbal Hallucinations."

Ella didn't add that she'd studied AVH because she herself sometimes heard voices.

"We found that delivering electrical pulses to the TPJ caused patients to hear less voices in their minds."

"Huh."

"And the Right TPJ," she tapped above and behind her right ear. "Is specialized. The main job for this region is to think about other people's thoughts."

Oliver's eyes darted from her face to her t-shirt and back.

Once again, Ella felt uncomfortable being alone with this large teenage boy. She folded her arms over her chest.

"The Right TPJ activates when you're putting yourself in someone else's shoes. When you're trying to understand what they might be thinking. So you can predict what they might do."

Her phone alarm plinged, reminding her to call Jady, and for once she appreciated being interrupted from her work.

"Let's take a break. I've got to make a call."

She closed the door behind Oliver and dialed her daughter on the bedside hotel phone.

Jady answered, her voice flat. "Hi, Mum."

"Hi, sweetie. Why didn't you answer my calls or texts?"

“I dunno. I’m really busy, Mum.”

Ella’s stomach tightened. She knew Jady was on autumn holiday.

“Well, look, sorry I couldn’t come home, but we’ve had a major breakthrough. These monks are showing a unique brain—”

“That’s awesome. Hey, Dad says I need your permission to get a tattoo.”

“What?”

Ella wondered if that meant her ex-husband, George had been okay with it.

“Becca and I are getting tattoos. I’m thinking of three little birds on my ankle—”

“No! No you’re not.”

Time for another discussion with Victoria about her daughter Becca’s influence.

“Did your father say you could?”

Jady made a groaning sound.

“I’m fifteen, Mum. The birds mean that I’m spreading my wings. It’s inspirational.”

Ella moved her head to fight a rising sense of vertigo.

“What do you care anyway?”

“Jady, I’ll be home this weekend and we can talk about this.”

A pause.

“Are you there?” Ella said.

“I got an “A” on my physics paper.”

“Well done. That’ll make up for your midterm mark.”

Another pause.

"No really," Ella said, "I'm proud of you Jady."

"Dad helped me. We were up most of the night."

"Oh."

Ella knew she shouldn't resent George for being such a caring father.

"Well, still, good for you," Ella said. "I did the same thing. One time, your mormor stayed up with me all night to finish my biology paper."

"Mormor?" Jady said, as if not believing her quiet grandmother could accomplish much of anything.

"She was brilliant."

"So, can I get the tattoo?"

"No." Ella wondered how they'd gotten back to that question. "I already said no."

Jady groaned again.

"I have to go. I'm staying at Becca's while Dad's gone."

"Check in with me tonight," Ella said.

Jady said okay, in a way that conveyed she had no intention of checking in, and then ended the call.

Years of these calls ending abruptly hadn't made them any easier. Ella sighed as she put the receiver back in the cradle. Ignoring the crinkling paper of the monk brain images, she lay back on the bed and replayed their call in her mind.

It wasn't ideal, she knew, but Jady would be fine at Becca's while George traveled on business. She'd received an "A" in physics. It was her only weak subject. She'd sounded so proud.

Ella thought of the time when she'd been excited to show her parents her stellar biology grade but, hearing her mother crying, had eavesdropped outside her parent's bedroom door instead. The conversation she'd overheard had become etched in her mind.

"The decision's final," Ella's mother, Ingrid, had said.

Ella knew immediately. Her mother hadn't been picked as the new conductor of the Stockholm orchestra.

"But how? You're the best," her father, Anders, had said. "Chauvinist bastards."

"No, it was me. I was terrible."

"Impossible. They can't do this. I'll—"

"No, no, Anders. I missed cues, my pacing was off. I was too tired to think straight."

Ella remembered her stomach dropping at that point, her gut figuring it out before her brain.

"Too tired?" her father said.

"I was up all the night before helping Ella with a paper."

Her mother's weeping sounded muffled, as if her face were buried in her father's shirt.

Ella remembered feeling dizzy in the hallway at that moment, a shifting inside her.

Her father released a loud, exasperated sigh. After a time, he said in a deep voice, which to young Ella sounded like the voice of God, "You can't be everything, my love."

Ella had crept back to her room; she didn't have the heart to show her grades. After that day, she'd watched her parents more closely.

Her mother cried when they visited the symphony, but never spoke of her loss. She never stopped being there for Ella, even though Ella rarely asked her for school help anymore. Ella's father, a prominent neurology professor at Stockholm University, only came home to sleep and eat. He was quiet except when asked about his work—in those moments, he lit up.

From these examples, Ella learned from both of her parents that succeeding in your career meant prioritizing it over everything else.

She rolled onto her side, crumpling more MRI print outs, and stared at the picture on her bedside table. It was a photo of Jady at five years old. She was sleeping peacefully, hair matted on her forehead and clutching her pink blanket, the tag up to her nose. Ella remembered those precious minutes, before she'd sneak out for the early train, when she'd spoon her warm little girl, smell her hair and, if she closed her eyes, feel as if they were one, safe from the world. It had been on a morning like that when she'd been convinced that she stopped Jady's hiccups by sending comforting thoughts.

Their relationship had been wonderful, or at least fine, until three years ago when she'd become Research Fellow and Associate Professor of Neuroscience at the University of Oxford. Remarkable for a thirty-seven-year-old woman, her father had said.

Unfortunately, the job came with an hour and a half commute each way from their flat in London. Jady was old enough to know that Ella's absence caused the divorce and, as a result, had been much harder on Ella than she was on her father. Yes, the mother-teenage-daughter dynamic was usually tough, but Ella knew she could only blame herself for her and Jady's complete disconnection.

Ella felt the tears rolling down the side of her face and realized that she was probably ruining the already crumpled print outs. What was going on? She asked herself. She had publishable findings from her year-long study and she had only tomorrow to draft a synopsis for Wendell, her department head, before she had to work on the app project the rest of the week.

She had to pull herself together.

###

Jon shuffled a few feet forward in the tightly winding customs line of Paro International Airport in Bhutan. As expected, the twenty-six-hour journey had been utterly exhausting. Beyond the bad air, the bad food and the bad sleep, the sensory overload and constant battle against interacting with anyone had been harder than ever before. Usually, by avoiding talking to people or making eye contact with them, he could cringe his way through crowds without experiencing other people's emotions.

But even while seated on the plane with his eyes closed, his mood had swung wildly, with bizarre mashups of conflicting emotions. He had to hurry and meet with Neema, he thought, because it felt like he was getting worse, more open.

He remembered how, years ago, he'd played games with his ability, like predicting how people were feeling before interacting with them or striking up conversations with happy-looking people so that he could feel happy himself. Unfortunately, he often found they were faking it or medicated, and he'd end up just confused.

His therapists had suggested that his condition was simply a matter of him noticing non-verbal cues in others and then empathizing in the traditional sense. This theory couldn't explain how he experienced the emotions of people by merely thinking about them. Eventually, he'd stopped playing games, accepted he was different, and tried to be a functioning, lonely adult. Like most of his eye-gazing clients.

Jon was alternating his stare between the ceiling and floor, when a young Asian man bumped into him as he was coming the other way in the snaking line. The man apologized, caught Jon's eye, and a connection was triggered. Jon wasn't concerned about entering Bhutan or authority figures in general. But the young man must have been, for the closer they got to the officials, the heavier the weight on Jon's chest became.

Wiping his brow, Jon gave a brave, tight-lipped smile to the security guard, telling himself to be more careful, or he'd never make it through this project.

Thirty minutes later, in the white resort van, his two traveling companions happy and relaxed, Jon could finally breathe. He sat in the front seat, swaying with the turns and playing his hand in the wind like a little boy as they meandered up the Paro Valley. Pine forests blanketed the steep hills on either side and rice paddies lined the river they followed.

The driver's name, Jigme, matched his giggly disposition, and his sun-burnished skin and betel-nut-stained teeth matched his red and brown uniform. Terry from Ft. Lauderdale, a kind-looking woman in her mid-fifties, had also traveled here for the app. She seemed content to hum the Adele song "Hello from the Other Side" to herself in the backseat, as if trying to make a point.

Jigme proudly recited his lines. "Bhutan is the world's last Buddhist kingdom. One of the most remote and pristine places on Earth." He pointed through the windshield. "Mt. Chomolhari, twenty-four thousand feet. We are at seven thousand feet now."

Jon swigged his water to stave off an altitude headache.

"We measure Gross National Happiness, not Gross Domestic Product." Jigme turned and gave a red-toothed grin as proof. They turned right into a smaller, narrower valley that seemed vaguely familiar to Jon from his childhood visit. "Taktsang Valley," Jigme said. "You visit Tiger's Nest?"

Jon replied yes and thought how he wanted to live there.

"Thirteen hundred years ago," Jigme said, "Guru Rinpoche, the second Buddha, flew from Tibet on the back of a tigress and meditated for three years in a cave on the cliff. Where the monastery now stands."

Jon had heard the legend before. This time he felt a strange sense of kinship, an unfamiliar desire to do something equally bold.

They came through a new-looking stone gate that read Nalu Resort. The smooth driveway wound up in sharp switchbacks and on one turn, Jigme stopped to point across a steep ravine. "Nalu, the newest five-star resort in Bhutan."

White buildings spread across the opposite hill, half hidden in a pine forest. Jon counted about twenty cabins in two rows above a cluster of larger structures.

Jigme pointed up through the windshield.

"At the top of the ridge is the resort bar. You can see Tiger's Nest on the far side of the next valley from there."

Snowcapped peaks of the Himalayas rose in the distance and a warm breeze carried the scent of the pines from the valley. Jon thought how he could definitely relax, maybe even be himself here. And with Tiger's Nest within hiking distance, it was perfect.

He could do this.

That evening, he waited in the lobby for dinner, groggy from his nap, and considered whether his mild anxiety came from himself or Terry. Just in case, he focused his attention on the small orange and black striped birds in the ornate aviary that dominated the center of the square room. The sign told him they were accentors, the local songbird. They flapped frantically about in the wire cage, as if desperate to escape.

A loud clomping on the wooden floor made him turn. There, striding toward him in calf-high leather combat boots and short-shorts, was a very fit woman, probably in her early thirties, her face set. Most striking though were the two large black holsters hanging from her belt, each strapped to her bare thighs.

She shook Jon's hand with what must have been everything she had.

"Alexandra Moller. Call me Lex."

Jon introduced himself, and then, as she turned to grip poor Terry's hand, he took in the rest of Lex's costume-like appearance. A turquoise tank top revealed sturdy shoulders and arms like the CrossFit women who visited his yoga studio. Her long, braided black hair fell to a leather utility belt with three or four items hanging from it, including a long knife in one of the holsters and a khaki-colored handgun in the other.

She turned and caught him staring at her waist.

"My boss, Jeffrey, will be down any minute for dinner. He's wrapping up an important call."

Terry thanked her for bringing them there.

Jon reeled, as Lex's dark psyche began infecting him like an emotional contagion. As usual, the physical symptoms came first: his heart rate ramped up and caffeine-like jitters buzzed down to his fingertips. He knew how this dinner would go, and after traveling for twenty-six hours, he simply didn't have it in him. Thankfully, he'd had a lifetime of practice bowing out of social situations.

"I'm sorry, but I'm not feeling well. I'll have to see you all in the morning."

He turned and headed out of the lobby, toward the steps up the hill.

"What?" Lex said. She came after him, boots clomping again. "No way."

She caught up to him and grasped his forearm.

Jon instinctively twisted his arm free and faced her in the aikido ready stance: his weight lower, feet at right angles, hands down with fingers splayed open

She took a half step back, as if remembering he was a martial arts expert.

He felt an urge to fight, but held his aggression in check, knowing that urge was actually coming from Lex.

"We fly you here, give you a room, and you try to bail on dinner?"

"I really appreciate you bringing me here, but I have to go up now."

She narrowed her eyes as a smirk spread across her face.

"Whatever. But you better blow us away tomorrow."

Jon left the lobby and climbed the long wooden stairs that zig zagged up the steep slope, taking deep breaths and studying his surroundings to help let go of Lex's tension.

Tall pines crowded the hillside, their brown needles blanketing the ground, giving the property a shady but open feeling, the trunks like a maze of columns. He came upon an intersection with a stone path running sideways across the hill. Along this path, he spotted five cabins to his left and five to his right. The stairs continued up and he could see another row of larger cabins above.

All the buildings were in the traditional Bhutanese design: thick rammed earth walls with arched, ornate windows and decorated eaves. Each had a spectacular view of the valley below.

Missing dinner, he told himself, would give him the chance to explore the resort since he'd been too tired when he'd first arrived. He turned left, away from his cabin and eventually passed the spa with its burbling fountain and wind chimes. Further on, he heard a rumbling and came around a sharp corner to see a thirty-foot high waterfall booming onto a pile of boulders in a cloud of mist.

A young woman in a simple brown robe swept the path with what looked like a homemade broom of sticks. Before she sensed his presence and looked up, Jon turned and headed back.

When he came to the intersection of stairs again, he turned left to climb further up the hill. Through the tree trunks, he counted six of the larger cabins, three on each side, each with a generous wooden deck jutting out. At the top of the stairs, signs pointed left for a plunge pool, mediation huts, and the Nalu Bar so he headed that way.

As the path wound in front of the three large cabins, the hillside became steeper and the rush of the waterfall became louder. He rounded a corner, and on his right, steps led further up the hill to the

Nalu Bar. At that point, the path before him became a narrow ledge carved out of the steep, rocky hill.

He continued on, cool mist gusting onto his face from up ahead, and as the hillside became a cliff, he was glad for the metal railing, even if it was a bit low. Soon the path curved and opened up onto a patio next to a large natural pool, surrounded on three sides by towering, sheer walls of gray stone.

Two thatched huts stood on stilts above the dark water, and beyond them, in the gloomy back, a ten-foot waterfall cascaded down. The plunge pool had a distinct current and to his left, boulders ran along the lip of the main waterfall to keep guests from tumbling over the edge.

He'd reached a dead-end. It felt like a natural temple, a secluded sanctuary, and he knew he'd be back here often. He followed the railing to the first of the boulders and the view was spectacular: the lush valley, the spa complex and the water crashing down onto the rocks below. A wave of exhaustion came over him—perhaps from the sound of the water—and he decided to head back down.

Jon's cabin was perched directly above Beyul, the indoor/outdoor restaurant. Not that anyone in his position could complain about his accommodations. Once Person8 had selected him as a finalist, they'd acquired him a visa and covered all his expenses.

He settled onto a cushioned lounge chair on his balcony, careful not to be seen by anyone below. He'd read in the lobby that according to Buddhist beliefs, Beyul was the term for hidden valleys where the physical and spiritual worlds overlapped. Looking over the peaceful vista, he thought how this place did have an ancient, spiritual feel to it.

The smell of rich, spicy food wafted up the bustling terrace and he realized how hungry he was. He should go down to eat, he thought. Plus, he really needed to be talking with the Person8 people, doing everything he could to get picked over Terry for this project.

A burst of laughter and cheers came from below, so he snuck to the rail to have a look. A large Asian family beamed at an old man trying to feed a baby. Jon pulled his gaze away and spotted a woman his age, alone at the bar, thumbing through her phone. She looked oddly familiar, and beautiful. He could go down and have a drink with her right now, he told himself. After all, he'd dated beautiful women before, only casually of course.

She put her phone on the bar and finished her drink.

He couldn't take his eyes off her.

She began folding, twisting her straw.

Jon presumed she was stressed about something, so he ducked back to his chair before he could absorb it, reminding himself to minimize any kind of connection and deciding to order room service.

A man's booming voice rose above the din below.

"To Tuning In!"

Tuesday, October 16

Jeffrey Venn was firing off his daily status update to Max Harding on video conference.

"Code's through QA and ready to rock. Choosing the spokesperson today, probably the woman. Our scientist will record her and make the tracks later today or first thing tomorrow. Then we add the tracks to the app and upload it to the app stores. Should be live the following day."

"Wednesday the 17th," Harding said.

"Wednesday in New York, Thursday in Bhutan. A lot of time zones. Anyway, on promotion, the videographer gets here from Mumbai tomorrow afternoon. So, we have time to revise the scripts if I pick the guy psychic today."

"Flying psychics to Bhutan to shoot videos." Harding grunted. "You are so completely over the top on this one."

"Hey, I said we're going big this year. Making it real."

"Whatever. You send me this guy's bio?"

"Jon Gunnarson. I'll send it again. He's a freak. Blew me off for dinner last night."

"He sounds pretty smart to me."

"Ha. Moving on, PR's looking solid. *The Guardian*, the *Times* and *CNN* are ready when we are."

"Riding the retard wave," Harding said, referring to the autistic girl in LA who'd proven her telepathic ability.

"I sent you the paid media test plan. You want the top line?"

"What do you think? Got your spreadsheet open."

Venn aimed his finger at Lex, sitting across the table.

"Okay," she said and cleared her throat. "We went over audience segments yesterday so, go to the second tab, called launch media. You can see it's front-loaded, with heavy paid inclusion on Facebook and saturating properties like Oprah and Chopra."

She paused for a moment.

Harding murmured, "Uh-huh."

"We'll finalize our ad units and paid search copy once we choose the spokesperson. Also, we've signed orders for the initial buys. Six hundred thousand for the first three days. We'll ramp it up once we've optimized to the target ROI."

"You're giving this a full year in the market?" Harding had obviously clicked to final tab of the sheet showing the full business model. "Wasn't it six months before?"

Venn put his palm up to Lex to take back control of the call. "Yeah, but now we're telling people they need to listen to it for three months before they become telepathic. When the early adopters start complaining about not hearing anything, we can string them along for a few months by saying they need to be consistent, and that everyone's different. That some people need to do it longer."

"And the Russian team will keep the hope alive with stories of people becoming telepathic," Lex said.

"Exactly," Venn said.

Lex had spearheaded building a team of experts in the art of mass psychological manipulation known as Social Engineering. Trained bots and live human chatters used fake blogs and fake social media profiles to flood the Internet with what seemed like real word-of-mouth product endorsements.

"We're using the personas from our flat belly campaigns," Lex said. "We've got hundreds that will be perfect."

"Jeffrey, we get twelve months on this thing and I'll marry you."

Venn grimaced. "Three exes are enough for me."

"Hope this goes, man," Harding said.

"We'll stomp on it. Now, I gotta run."

"Hold a sec," Harding said. "Anything new from the FBI?"

"Not a peep. Meeting's a week from today. I fly back next Monday."

"What are they calling it?"

"I told you." Venn switched to a high voice, mocking the female FBI agent in charge. "An interview as part of our Internet fraud investigation."

"D.A. gonna be there?"

"I don't think so."

"No search warrant? Subpoena?"

"Max. Relax. It's nothing."

Venn ended the call and turned to Lex, who was busy on her laptop.

"We need to make this thing come screaming out of the gate."

# # #

Jon really wanted to ask what was with her outfit. But given the fact that this odd and somewhat frightening Lex woman's emotions were radiating off her like a furnace, he chose to wait quietly. He sat on a wooden dining chair in the middle of an otherwise nearly empty room, bracing for her inevitable outburst.

She'd been pacing in front of the window, hands on her hips, fingers tapping the tops of her fake leather holsters for almost five minutes. Her left boot creaked with each step, and he wondered why it wasn't driving her nuts as well.

The situation might have almost been comical if he hadn't desperately needed them to choose him over Terry as the spokesperson for the app project. His work visa depended on Person8, so he wouldn't be able to stay in Bhutan for more than a day or two if he wasn't selected. It seemed pretty hopeless to him at the moment.

He figured that whatever special ability he had was far too subtle to overcome her clear animosity towards him.

And what, exactly, was his special ability? he asked himself. Empathizing? It was surprising they'd even brought him here. Still, if he headed straight to Tiger's Nest after these interviews, he might be able to meet with Neema at least once before he had to fly home.

Lex came in front of him and leaned in. She put a finger to the middle of his chest. "You made me look really bad to Jeffrey Venn last night."

Jon struggled to resist her wave of heat.

She snapped open a holster and pulled out her gun. As she brought it upward he straightened, ready to reach for the weapon. She aimed it at his face and he noticed that the barrel wasn't a barrel at all, but a plastic rectangular opening with metal nubs on the top and bottom.

Jon eased, just slightly.

"You shouldn't be too relieved, Gunnarson. This is an M-26 Taser. The US military version of a commercial taser. Kinda surprised they let me bring it into the country."

She strolled behind him.

"It's got different settings. Like Drive Stun."

She made a humming, almost moaning sound.

"Really can't wait to use this thing."

Jon heard a clicking sound and resisted the urge to jump up.

"You ever been tasered, Jon?"

"No."

"Well, today could be your lucky day. What do you say we start this interview? Tell me, what am I thinking of right now?"

"You're thinking about tasering me."

"Wow, that's very good." She laughed. "You must be psychic."

After another silent, anxious minute, she pulled over another chair to sit across from him, crossed her legs, and folded her arms across her chest.

"We're supposed to what, stare into each other's eyes?"

"That's what I do with my clients."

Lex squinted but Jon could still see her eyes darting between his face, the walls, and the floor.

Her patience didn't last long.

"This is such bullshit. You're just sitting there. People pay you for this?"

Despite her impatience, she stayed in her seat.

Jon remained quiet, focused on the physical sensation of Lex's emotions in his body, alerting himself to the subtler nuances. It took a while, much longer than most new client sessions before he felt the shift in her. The shift that happened when clients seemed to subconsciously sense there was something going on. When they allowed themselves to participate.

Her counter stare steadied. As the minutes flew by, their breathing synchronized and their postures mirrored. Then her tears came.

Jon felt from her a strong self-loathing—a deep-seated doubt, jealousy, and insecurity—stronger than he'd ever felt before.

Eventually, a muted ding came from one of the pockets of Lex's belt, presumably signaling the end of their interview. She hunched over and rubbed her face.

Jon handed her a napkin; he'd thought ahead.

She blew her nose loudly and then examined what she'd expelled, as if reading invisible tea leaves. "What did you hear?"

Jon had learned that the best way to answer this question was directly.

"You don't like yourself and you're concerned about losing someone you care about."

"Fuck you, asshole." She stood and came up next to him, then paused. "I'd never let that happen." She traced her fingers across his cheek to his mouth, then pinched his lower lip, hard.

Jon jerked his head away and looked up to her in shock.

"That will be all," she said and smiled.

Standing at the corner of the Beyul restaurant terrace, Jon rolled his shoulders, trying to ease the tension. Lex had been relentless; unlike every other client, her rage and angst hadn't faded at all throughout the session.

She was like a bottomless pit, he thought. And a masochistic sociopath. Who he'd have to put up with all week if he somehow got selected.

He stretched his hands high over his head, leaned back to the expansive Himalayan sky, and put his face to the morning sun, hoping to come back to himself in the gentle reddish-orange world that lingered behind his eyelids.

Of course, Lex came instantly back to mind. Jon realized that she hadn't denied his reading, and he tried to imagine who could be in a relationship with someone like her. He also wondered who was making her so jealous.

Footsteps approached from behind.

Wanting just a minute of peace, he set his gaze forward, pretending to study the lush valley and snow-covered peaks beyond.

A woman came up next to him. As she said hello, a high-pitched tone suddenly filled his head and both his ears starting ringing.

Jon didn't know it, but the woman next to him was Ella Sandström, and her brainwave frequencies were uniquely complementary to his. When she came close to him, even the infinitesimally small force of her brainwaves was enough to interact with his in such a way as to accelerate the realignment of mirror neurons in his brain.

Glancing out the corner of his eye, a moment too late to see her face, he saw only her light brown hair and silk blouse. Must be another Person8'er, he thought and mumbled a hello back.

"It's like something from an inspirational calendar," she said, in an English accent.

The ringing continued, a wavering, impossibly high frequency whistling, as though he'd been near an explosion or was hearing dog whistles.

"Are you here for the app?" she said.

"Yeah." Jon opened his mouth wide and wiggled his jaw, but it didn't help.

"Are you one of the psychics?" Ella asked.

The noise in his head was overwhelming. He had to make it stop. "Sorry, I have to go." As he turned, he glimpsed her face and the insulted look in her piercing green eyes.

Walking back to the restaurant, he tried covering his ears, rubbing them to ease the high frequency tone. It made no difference; the sound didn't seem to be coming from his ears. It felt like it was coming from inside his head.

Great, he thought, just in time for my main interview.

He'd never experienced something like this before and wondered what it could be, what could have caused it. He realized it had started when that woman came next to him and he hoped it wasn't a new reaction to people, another new thing for him to deal with.

Jon shook his head one last time, tried to pull himself together, and reminded himself that his symptoms always started to subside once he took his attention off the other person. This will start fading any minute now, he assured himself.

"There you are," Lex said, poking her head out of the private dining room. "Jeffrey Venn will see you now."

"Telepathic?" Jon said.

"That's why you're here," Venn said, his eyes focused on his phone.

Jon noticed on the side table, a utility belt with holster, similar to Lex's and thought how they must have bought a matching set. How cute.

"Your clients say you feel what they feel, take away their negative feelings," Venn said, reading from his screen. "That sometimes it seems like you know what they're thinking, even though you don't talk with them."

The whistling tone continued, and, on top of it, Jon felt Venn's pull, like a magnet or a heavy weight. He knew he should say something, but all he could do was take a breath to try and slow his pulse.

"Telepathy's hot right now," Venn said, finally putting his phone down.

Thankfully, Jon thought, this guy didn't seem to mind doing all the talking.

"Have you heard of sentiment analysis?"

Jon shook his head, trying not to wince.

"My advertising clients need to know what people think of their brands. That's why my agency listens to billions of online conversations. Then we use a powerful algorithm and a team in India to fix mistakes from slang, context, ambiguity, and sarcasm. Gets us to about eighty percent accurate."

As Venn described his area of expertise, Jon felt the heaviness coming from him ease slightly.

"*My* magic's real," Venn said. "I can use sentiment analysis for any topic. I know what people are thinking. And for some reason a lot of people are thinking about telepathy right now." He moved his gaze to the window as if something had caught his eye. "Tell me, Gunnarson, what am I thinking of right now?"

He followed Venn's gaze out the window and saw the woman who'd joined him on the terrace moments earlier.

Venn grunted, like he'd just bitten into a cheeseburger.

Jon watched her approach and could easily guess what Venn was thinking. Once he saw her face, he realized she was the woman sitting at the Beyul bar last night. He snapped himself out of it, remembering that Venn had asked him to read his mind.

"It's not like that."

Venn turned back and leaned in. "No? So, what's it like? Enlighten me."

"Well, I connect with a client and sense an area of difficulty in their life, like a relationship or their career. Based on my experience in working with lots of people, I give a kind of guidance. People say it's pretty close to their reality."

"You connect with a client." Venn steepled his hands, looking like a stock photo titled, Businessman Thinking. "What does that mean exactly?"

"I don't know, but I feel what they're feeling," Jon said. "Maybe I'm good at reading body language."

"And how do you give guidance if you don't talk?"

"I'm not sure. With my eyes?"

"With your eyes. You give guidance with your eyes."

"Possibly. I'm not really sure how any of it happens."

A drop of sweat ran down from his armpit, a reminder of how desperately he needed this job.

Venn flicked his laptop shut and sat up.

"Okay, well if you're so perceptive, then you must know how this meeting went. It's too bad, Lex wanted you. She loved that picture of you here as a kid." He raised his voice to a high pitch, mocking her. "The spiritual soccer moms will love him."

Jon heard Lex force a laugh in the adjoining dining room. He felt a pit in his stomach and began inspecting his hands.

"But before I send you home, let's have a go. You and me. Pretend I'm one of your clients. I'll even give you a hint. Career challenges. We can talk about my love life another time." Venn winked.

Jon felt a headache coming on and with the room quiet, the whistling seemed louder. He focused on his breathing. Given his years of practice, he was able to go deeply inward, even while holding Venn's gaze.

Venn darted his attention around Jon's face for a minute before settling into a steady counter stare.

Jon felt the familiar shift as his mind became still. The room around him slipped away and he saw only Venn's dark eyes. A powerful fist tightened in Jon's chest. This was different, deeper. He took quick, shallow breaths, staying with it as best he could. The minutes sped by and his body vibrated, as if he were being shocked.

Jon had felt this type of emotion before—a nasty blend of fear, anxiety and shame—and knew it often came from pending catastrophic career failure. He swayed in his seat, feeling more than he'd ever felt before from a client.

After a time, Venn's eyes watered, and he looked away. "Okay. That's enough." He stood and moved to look out the window. "What did you hear?"

Jon said whatever words came to him. "You want to prove you still have it."

"Ha. Like anyone turning fifty. But go ahead."

"You really want this project to succeed. To show you're still in touch. That you're not over the hill and can make big things happen. You'll do whatever it takes." Jon closed his eyes. "But this project's not your real challenge. You could lose your company. Your freedom."

"Okay, that's enough."

Venn came back to the table and gathered up his phone and laptop.

"You certainly have quite the imagination. But people eat that shit up."

He pulled a manila envelope from his laptop bag.

"The contract. You get one percent of net revenue and it caps at twenty thousand. If you don't like it, we'll go with Terry and you can fly home tomorrow. If you sign it, you head up to Tiger's Nest for photos. I need an answer in an hour."

Venn left the room without another glance in Jon's direction.

Pulling a dense-looking legal document from the envelope, Jon tried to imagine what kind of danger Venn and Person8 could be in.

The danger seemed imminent, which meant this app may never hit the market and he wouldn't earn a dime.

He skimmed the contract, the clauses on his promotional obligations stretching to three pages, and then swooped his signature at the end, knowing he would have signed almost anything to stay in Bhutan to meet with Neema.

Now he just needed to hear back from her. He needed to know if a visit was even possible. Because if he couldn't meet with her, this whole traumatic experience would be for nothing.

Regardless, he was about to head up to Tiger's Nest. Despite the whistling tone and headache, the notion lifted his spirits. Because he knew that in a place like that, anything could happen.

Less than an hour later, Jon watched the road ahead while Jigme, the same driver from the day before, swerved the resort van down the valley, away from the resort, and then around the ridge toward the Tiger's Nest parking lot. Jon kept his gaze forward to avoid motion sickness, and also to avoid Lex, who sat close and facing him on the bench seat.

"We'll do photos first, then a quick video," she said. "Unscripted, totally natural. Just talk about your telepathy. You'll do great."

"I don't have telepathy."

"Well, this is a telepathy app and you're the spokesperson. Hell, it's gonna be *based* on you, you're like the father of it. So we're gonna have to stretch the truth here."

She squeezed his shoulder in authority and Jon fought the urge to shrug her off.

"Now, we'll need to find the exact spot you posed with your mother. We should take it together, so you're not alone," she said, tapping his forearm now. "I'll stand on your right, like she did."

Jon could hardly take a breath. He wasn't sure if his tension came from Lex, who was wound up on self-hatred, caffeine, stress and sexual attraction, or from himself. After all, he was about to demean his best childhood memory of his mother.

"You're the strong silent type, aren't you?" she said.

He would have corrected her to say he was more of the overwhelmed reclusive type with an insane whistling piercing his skull, but she kept talking.

"I like that," she said, her hand back on his shoulder. "My shrink says I need a more reserved man so that I can shine through."

Jigme swung into a large parking lot and announced their arrival.

Jon leapt from the van and busied himself helping Jigme unpack small black cases of camera and lighting gear. He loaded up with four cases, some of them heavy, and Lex took the remaining two. They walked a quarter of a mile up a gentle slope to reach the base of the trail.

Lex was clearly a strong woman, but she was already winded in the altitude. When she learned that she faced a strenuous, four-hour round-trip trek up to ten thousand feet, she demanded mules or horses or *something* to carry them up the mountain.

Jon let her know he needed the exercise, and to his huge relief, she agreed to meet him near the top. He headed toward the trail alone, Lex's tension dissipating by each step.

Creaking wooden prayer wheels caught his attention. As he spun one, he remembered his mother's gentle reproach from years ago. "They're not toys, Jon," she'd said.

His mom, Hanna Magnúsdóttir, had taken to her roommate's religion at the University of Iceland, becoming one of the rare Buddhists in the country at the time. Years later, she'd heard that a Buddhist monk from Tiger's Nest was visiting Reykjavik, and she'd brought her seven-year-old son, Jon, to demonstrate their deep connection. Hanna didn't like the word telepathy but admitted that she and her son tapped into each other's minds. The monk had been stunned and had invited them to come to the monastery.

They'd visited for nine days, rising before dawn to meditate, chant, sing, and study sutras. Jon had performed to a roomful of rapt monks, correctly naming numbers or letters his mother held on cards in another room. Asked to describe his experience, he could only stammer that he saw pictures from what he called the bigger mind.

A gonging bell brought him back to the present.

Time to hike. He took a deep breath of pine mountain air and set off, the sun warm on his back, carrying only his metal water bottle. He began with his usual style of bounding up the trail, but soon felt winded, exhausted even, and slowed his pace, shocked at how much the altitude was affecting him.

Alone with his thoughts for the first time in hours, Jon finally had a chance to study the high frequency tone that persisted in his head. The pitch fluctuated constantly within a narrow range that went up, down, steady, down, up, up, down. There didn't seem to be any pattern, which made it even harder to ignore, like a madman playing a harmonica made of dog whistles in his head. The tone distracted him from most of his thoughts, but he kept putting one foot in front of the other and after ninety minutes came to a turn in the path directly across from the monastery.

It clung impossibly to the opposite wall of a deep chasm, a sheer cliff. Four temples and two tall, narrow dormitories behind them clustered like haphazard steps on the narrow granite ledges. The buildings had white walls with red-maroon bands around their tops. Delicate maroon and gold patterns ornamented the windows, and the roofs were nearly flat with large overhanging eaves. He stood slightly higher than the monastery and saw that while the roofs of the lower levels were maroon, the three layers of cupolas stacked on top of the square main temple had gilded copper roofs that shone a beautiful gold in the sun.

Prayer flags fluttered on lines across the chasm like colorful square bits of laundry. And to his left, where the two cliffs came together, a three-hundred-foot waterfall cascaded, billowing mist.

It was quite the view.

He steadied himself in the wind and peered down into the two-thousand-foot abyss. It was dizzying. Not something you'd want to mess with, he thought, that's for sure.

Jon had read everything he could find about Tiger's Nest and knew this was where Buddhism began in Bhutan. For at least thirteen hundred years, pilgrims had traveled and climbed to meditate here. Every day, visitors left with new accounts of visions and spiritual awakenings. One of his favorite legends was how Guru Rinpoche had the habit of simultaneously appearing both inside and outside his cave while directing work on the foundation for the buildings.

He considered how people found places of peace and power in the world and built magical structures like this one or Stonehenge, or the Easter Island Statues, the Great Pyramids or Angkor Wat. It was as if they sensed something vital was happening there, like a harmonic energy, a portal to transcendence.

Birds sang behind him, the same accentor birds from the lobby and he turned, looking back the way he'd come. From this high perspective, he spotted the Nalu Resort Bar, a fresh, perfectly square gash on the ridge. He saw how someone could hike along that ridge, and meet the monastery trail about halfway up, saving fifteen hundred feet in elevation and miles of trail. A shortcut.

He studied the route for landmarks and decided to try it when he came back to meet with Neema—if he came back. He'd mailed a letter to her at Tiger's Nest, informing her of his travel plans and asking for a meeting. He hadn't heard back. He considered that with no devices of any kind and her near constant travel, she wouldn't be the fastest, most reliable communicator.

He settled on a rock, staring at the monastery, and remembering the first time he'd met Neema here over thirty years ago. She was a radiant young Tibetan woman back then. The monks considered her to be the human medium for the Tenma Oracle, the physical basis for the guardian goddesses of Buddhism. The Dalai Lama had found her advice so valuable that he often brought her with him on his travels. At the age of eighteen, she'd seen the world and had discovered aikido while in Japan.

She and Jon had spun and twisted in the monastery's congregation hall for hours every day, his mother outside gazing at the breathtaking view to avoid distracting him. Neema had said he could be a rokudan someday.

Cold mist from the waterfall brought him back to the present. He should be a rokudan right now, he thought. Still, he'd made it here. It felt like things were coming together, as if the universe were scheming on his behalf.

He spotted a pair of pilgrims coming down from Tiger's Nest, holding a rickety handrail as they navigated steps carved into the exposed cliff face. They were a young couple, babies wrapped snug on their backs.

A gust of wind enveloped them in mist. Jon rose, craning his neck to find them. The vapor cleared and they reappeared, closer now. As they passed, they glanced his way, beaming with delight.

Jon smiled back. He turned his gaze back across the chasm and imagined Neema inside, meditating in one of the temples. He remembered the first time he'd watched her in a shaking trance, staring at nothing. If anyone could help him understand and manage his strange condition, it was Neema. And she was right there.

Yes, he thought, Lex would arrive on her mule and he'd pose for the camera, even betray the memory of his dead mother. Because it felt like this was where he needed to be, where he was meant to be.

Wednesday, October 17

Jon climbed the steps after breakfast, to the luxury "Arama" level, his calves tight from his hike the day before. He made his way to the correct cabin and studied it as he caught his breath. It looked more like a small house. A column of steam rose from behind. Three crows eyed him from the gutter.

He pictured the scientist inside, hustling around, and realized that he actually had no idea what to expect; he'd only been given a time and a cabin number for his appointment. Venn and Lex, so meticulous about promotional tasks, had treated his brainwave recording session almost as an afterthought. But to Jon, whoring his brainwaves felt about on par with debasing himself on camera.

You have to do this, he told himself.

He stepped forward, knocked, and heard footsteps approaching from inside. The door swung in and there was the woman from the terrace.

The woman from the video.

He felt a slight shift, as though the earth had paused a moment.

"Jon Gunnarson?" The expression in her pale green eyes reminded him that he'd been a bit rude on the terrace. She leaned out to shake his hand. "I'm Ella Sandström."

Ella Sandström. He still had the screenshot of her on his phone. Humbled by the scale of this coincidence, by the sheer audacity of it, he could only shake her hand and nod.

"Let's do this," she said, and turned to lead him into the room.

Jon noticed her snug, faded jeans and quickly brought up his gaze. She'd grown her hair back and she was probably ten years older. But this was the woman from the video.

The aroma of freshly brewed coffee filled the tall, open space, and the warm sun streamed in the floor-to-ceiling windows on the far wall. A keyboard clicked to his left, and he turned to see a teenager surrounded by a mini computer lab, his head nodding to the beat of his headphones.

"My assistant, Oliver Mabry," Ella said.

Jon moved into Oliver's field of vision and the boy jumped up, bumping the underside of the table with his thigh and nearly toppling the desk lamp.

"Oliver, this is Jon Gunnarson," Ella said. "Our subject for the app project."

"Good to meet you. I'm pre-med at London University."

"You too," Jon said, not sure if Oliver's thick black frames and red t-shirt with the word SKRILLEX scrawled across the front made him a hipster or a geek.

"You'll sit there," she said to Jon, pointing to a low wooden chair.

Jon sat dutifully.

Ella came on one knee in front of him, holding a bramble of white plastic circles, each attached to thin white wires that all fed into a thick cord.

She had a wild look. Scandinavian features on a stress diet. Sensual and ravenous. Jon took a breath, surprised to find his chest wide open.

"This is a geodesic net." She used both hands to untangle the net into the shape of a cap and came close to fit it on his head. "Two hundred and fifty-six sensors."

The whistling tone became downright fierce, and he shook his head. As usual, it didn't help.

Ella pulled back, her eyes asking, *Are you okay mate?*

Jon knew the look all too well. He nodded.

"I just slip this on, alright?" Her hands opened inside the net and she brought it onto Jon's hair, brushing his ears and his neck as she fitted the complex mesh onto his head.

It felt like a bead headdress. Jon realized he hadn't said more than two words since arriving. "How does it work?"

Ella spoke as she put the sensors in place. "Neurons generate electric currents. When lots of neurons act together, like when you focus your attention, they make neural oscillations, or brainwaves. We detect that movement with this EEG."

Her British accent made her sound especially brilliant.

"I measure seven categories of brainwaves. Each has a different frequency and amplitude range and each correlate with different mental states. For example, my experiments with monks show a correlation between transcendence and high frequency gamma waves."

She bent over and patted around the cap, as though styling his hair, her necklace dangling before his nose.

Jon had a clear view into her shirt. He closed his eyes.

"Today," Ella said. "We'll use digital EEG to record your brainwaves in different states like alert, calm, meditative. Then you're done. After you go, we'll use these computers to amplify the brainwaves thousands of times and then run them through the latest algorithms. This will give us a complete copy of how your brain is firing."

Jon wondered if he should mention that it sounded like truck brakes were squeaking in his head.

"Well, I better think nice thoughts then."

Ella gave the hint of a smile. The same smile that had captivated him two weeks earlier.

"Not actual thoughts," she said, arranging sensors on his face, "Only how your neurons are firing."

"Got it."

"The last step is transposing that copy of your brainwaves into binaural beats for the app soundtrack."

"Binaural beats?"

She knelt again, to set a sensor in between his eyebrows, and her fingers skimmed his face.

"Here's how it works. If you hear a different frequency in each ear, your brain creates its own third signal—a binaural beat—equal to the difference between the two frequencies. And, what's amazing, is that your brain follows this new signal."

Jon raised his brows, feeling the weight of the sensors.

"So, I could put anyone into the slow, sleepy delta state by playing a five hundred hertz tone in their left ear, and a five hundred and two hertz tone in their right ear. Their brain would create a frequency pulsing at two hertz and then resonate with it. It's called brainwave entrainment." Ella paused, transfixing him with her eyes.

"Oh, right," he managed. "It works, huh?"

"Absolutely. I've been doing entrainment for years and my brain maps have changed quite a bit."

"Neuroplasticity," Jon said, pulling the word up from grad school and winning himself another small Ella smile.

"Very good. We can change the circuitry of our brains. Although, that's old news and people have been creating computer-generated binaural beats for years. This new program creates tracks based on exact replicas of amplitude and frequency for an individual's specific brain region. For this app, we're going to replicate your right TPJ region."

Jon nodded, thinking how he must look ridiculous.

"So, over time, a few days, weeks, or months depending on how their brains are wired, if people listen to the recording every day, the neurons in their TPJ regions will rearrange to connect exactly as yours do. The track we create will put listeners' brains in the same exact state as your brain."

"I wonder," Jon said. "If there'd be a way to change my brain so that I'm not so—" he paused, "sensitive. You know, picking up what other people are feeling? My gift is my curse?"

Ella didn't seem to get the Spiderman reference and gave him the *are-you-okay* look again. "I think that's why you're here though, right?"

Her eyes shifted up to scan his scalp. She leaned in close to re-stick the sensors behind his right ear, their heads almost touching.

The close interaction of their brainwaves triggered further realignment of the mirror neurons in Jon's brain. He felt a strange shuddering sensation, like a tremor or low electric shock in his head.

He brought up his hand.

"What's that shaking?"

Ella straightened and frowned.

"You shouldn't feel anything. These are only sensors. And I haven't even plugged them into the amp yet."

The shuddering in his head faded away, but the high-pitched whine had cranked up a notch. As usual, he tried to figure out if the feeling originated from himself or from another person. This had started when she first came next to him on the terrace, he thought. No, she couldn't be feeling this; no one could live like this.

"Okay, this is completely painless. Close your eyes, keep still and don't move your eyes or blink. Try to stay calm."

Jon noticed that despite everything, he'd felt unusually calm since he'd walked in the door.

She moved to her workstation and typed in commands. "Now, for your first meditation, try to create a state of deep compassion."

He'd committed his sensei's words to memory. "An unrestricted readiness and availability to help living beings."

"Exactly. If you can."

Jon heard in her voice another smile, and he also knew, he somehow *knew* she'd just smiled.

He felt so deeply connected with this woman that it seemed as if he'd been brought to Bhutan not to learn from Neema, but to meet Ella. Which was not his plan at all.

Jon left Ella's cabin an hour later in a sort of happy trance. The sun was warming the hillside and he inhaled the pine mountain air. He wanted nothing more than to go running up the mountain, but knew he was already late for his media training with Lex.

Walking the short distance to Lex's cabin next door, he thought back to his interview with her and their video session from the day before. Which Lex would he get today? he wondered. Would she be the bully or the flirt? Hopefully his happy, transcendent state could withstand either of them.

When Lex answered the door in a red bikini, Jon had his answer.

"Come on in. I was in the hot tub."

Her cabin had the same layout as Ella's. He followed her through the big open room and out the sliding glass doors onto the deck. A hot tub churned, and two lounge chairs lay side by side, almost touching. He could plainly see Ella's cabin and deck to his left and, about thirty yards away on his right, Venn reclined on his own deck, phone to his ear as usual.

Lex sat and tapped the adjacent chair. "Sit here."

Jon sat and instantly wanted to slide his chair apart from hers.

She turned on her side to face him, her face serious. "Let's keep this casual today, make it fun."

Her hot rage started seeping into him.

"I need you to open up to me completely, so we can come up with some story lines that will make those spiritual soccer moms love you."

This was going to be a long day, Jon thought.

"First, do you have a girlfriend?"

"No."

"Why not? You're a hot guy. You don't seem gay."

"No. It's just that I get too close."

"Huh. Okay, so what do you like to do?"

"Aikido, trail running, mountain biking, yoga."

Lex sat up, flicked her eyes past him to Venn's cabin.

"I have an idea. Stay there."

She strutted inside.

The hot tub jets whirred, the tone in his head whistled, and an insect ticked, hidden somewhere behind him.

Jon sat up and grabbed a plum from the side table. He bit into the tart skin, the sweet flesh.

Lex returned and headed to the far edge of the deck, holding a camera. “Okay, come over here. And take off your shirt.”

Jon felt a bit silly but figured it was better than her threatening him with a taser. So he did as he was told. For the next five minutes, she photographed him in various yoga poses. While her stress and anger remained, he also felt her rising desire. And as with Danielle two weeks before, he couldn’t help but become aroused as well.

“Warrior-two,” she said, glancing over to Venn’s deck again.

Jon transitioned his body, his left thigh at a ninety-degree angle, his right leg straight behind him and his arms outstretched.

She came close and touched his arms to turn him slightly.

He now stared over his fingertips directly at Venn on the other deck.

“There,” she said. “Better shadows on your chest and stomach. Very hot.”

He saw Venn glance over at them, then stand and go inside.

Lex crouched around Jon, taking pictures from every angle.

He tried not to think how his shorts must look.

“Okay, and reverse.”

Still bending his leg deeply, Jon lifted his forward arm up and back, his eyes closed as he faced the sun, feeling the stretch in the left side of his body.

Lex's hands were on him again, both of them, which meant she must have put down the camera.

"No, stay," she said. "Oh, your skin is so warm."

Jon felt himself becoming hard, and he thought how even though this woman was toxic, he soon wouldn't be able to control himself and they'd end up—

The door slid open with a swish. "How's the media training going?" Venn said.

Lex turned. "We're doing a photo shoot first."

Jon came out of the pose and adjusted himself.

Venn's eyes darted between them. "We need to get him ready for his interviews. The app launches tomorrow." He looked to Jon and spoke more sharply. "You can put your shirt on now."

Lex sighed, sashayed to the side table and squeezed a plum in the bowl.

Venn came behind her and spoke quietly, but just loud enough for Jon to hear.

"Love your bikini, Lara."

Jon pulled on his t-shirt and tried to make sense of what he'd heard.

"Be right back," Lex said, and left them.

Venn settled onto one of the lounge chairs.

"Sit down, Gunnarson. Let's talk."

Jon sat and leaned back, the two of them almost shoulder to shoulder.

"She's a city girl, going a bit stir crazy out here," Venn said. "She also likes to play games. It's flattering. But you gotta be careful not to get hurt."

Venn reached down and picked up some papers from the deck.

"Here we go. You ever deal with the press before?"

"No."

"Dealing with the media is like a fight. If you get a nasty question, you have to attack it and then pivot back to the message points. These are your message points. Study them. Practice in front of a mirror."

Lex came out to stand in front of them, the huge knife in her one hand and the taser in her other. She still sported her bikini but had added her boots and utility belt to her outfit. She looked like an action hero on vacation, Jon thought.

She pushed the end of Jon's chair aside then stepped between the two men, putting one boot up on Venn's chair and opening her knee wide. She leveled her taser inches from Jon's face and with her other hand, hovered the tip of the knife above Venn's lap. It was a dramatic pose.

"This what you had in mind?" she asked Venn.

In a few awkward and risky movements, Venn pulled her on top of him and she straddled his lap. Still holding her weapons, she leaned down and kissed him passionately.

Jon looked out over the valley, knowing he should get up and go, but the raw lust he was absorbing from them was so heavy, he felt as if he were pinned to the chair.

Lex put the taser down and groped Jon's chest.

Jon turned to see her looking at him with what might have been a smile.

Venn was biting at her neck, his hands on her grinding hips.

She slid her hand down onto Jon's stomach.

All at once, something deep inside of Jon broke free of her flooding desire. He was able to swing himself up out of the chair and stumble toward the door, half-expecting a taser shot to hit his back at any moment.

Once inside his own, smaller cabin, he shut the windows, sat on the corner of his bed, and closed his eyes. The whistling tone seemed even louder in the silence, and he wondered if he could still sit with the awful noise. He stayed with it, his thoughts shifting from his mind-blowing meeting with Ella to his bizarre experience with Lex and Venn. It was worth it, he reminded himself.

Was it really, though?

He had to fly home in a few days and Neema hadn't responded yet about when he could visit her. Even if she did, Venn and Lex wouldn't let him break free from his packed schedule of promotional videos and media interviews. He'd come all the way here and subjected himself to hours of stressful humiliation for nothing.

No. He decided that after lunch he'd just hike up there and hopefully Neema would see him. If Venn and Lex freaked out, so be it.

# # #

Ella sat at her desk, scrolling through screens of data. "Oh my God."

Oliver crowded beside her, silent behind his glasses.

"Look at this," she said. "His baseline's between thirty-three and thirty-eight hertz. That's high-beta, almost low-gamma. How could he maintain that state?"

"What do you mean?" Oliver asked.

"The high-beta band relates to complex thought, integrating new experiences, and high anxiety or excitement. Low-gamma's are associated with feelings of transcendence. I don't know how he could live like that. High frequency processing takes an enormous amount of mental energy."

"He did seem pretty quiet."

"He should be exhausted," she said. "And look. Here's his meditative state." She put her finger to the screen. "Forty-two hertz. That's high gamma. High even for our monks, guys who've meditated for fifty thousand hours over forty years."

"Gamma waves are for like, psychic powers and out of body experiences, right?"

Ella imagined Oliver's free time spent roaming the Internet. "We're still trying to understand gamma, but it may play a role in creating the unity of conscious perception."

Oliver scratched his chin, clearly confused.

"Okay, so when you see an object," Ella pointed to her phone. "Its color, size, sound, and smell are all perceived and processed by different parts of the brain. Gamma waves seem to unify all this different information, like a harmonizing frequency."

Oliver grunted, sounding like he understood, which he probably didn't.

"I'm not sure if we can even use this," Ella said. "I mean, can you entrain a brain at forty-two hertz?"

She opened a new window and tapped her finger to the screen again.

"Here's the activity map. His Right TPJ is all fired up."

She wished she still had the MRI truck. What a brain Jon had.

A dialog box popped up on her screen, notifying her that Jady was calling her on Skype. Jady was finally calling her back but as usual, at just the wrong moment. She opened the program and her daughter's image filled one of her screens.

Oliver rose to leave.

Ella waved him back down. "No, it's okay."

"Yeah, I don't have much time either," Jady said.

"Oh, sorry, I was talking to someone else. How are you, love?"

"Fine."

"How's autumn holiday coming?"

Ella flicked her gaze to her other screen to see if Jon's deep gamma state remained consistent over the full forty minutes. It did.

"Raining. Everyone except me and Becca are in Majorca."

"Well, that's good." Ella said, her voice flat and her eyes still on the data. "Are you going down to Brighton?"

"Dad can't."

The conversation paused.

"Mum, hello?"

Ella tore her focus away from the data. "Sorry, let me take this in the other room. Hold on." She unplugged her laptop from her monitor and carried it into her bedroom. Now intent on giving Jady her undivided attention, she sat on her bed, hunched over her laptop. "Hi, this is better. So, you talked with your father about the tattoo?"

"Yeah, whatever. It was more Becca's idea anyway." Jady looked down to her phone. "Hang on, this is dad."

While Jady spoke to her father, Ella had the chance to examine her daughter's black knit hat, pulled low over her eyebrows, and the purple smudges under her eyes. Somber, was the word that came to mind. From what Ella could see, Becca's room was a complete mess; layers of dirty clothes, fast food wrappers, and small cans of energy drinks littered every surface. Becca's mother, Victoria, put in long hours as the new CEO of a pharmaceutical company, and Ella doubted the girls were getting much supervision.

Jady seemed to be arguing with her father—she'd muted the Skype call, so Ella couldn't hear.

Ella considered what she should say when Jady came back on their call. What would the confident mothers she knew back in London say to their teenagers? They'd be understanding, but clear and firm.

"Hey, I'm back," Jady said, frowning.

"You said it was Becca's idea, but do *you* want a tattoo?"

"Yeah, I mean, I don't know," Jady said, as though she'd been asked a ridiculous question. "Peter thinks they're hot." Peter Osbourne attended Westminster School with Jady and his name had come up a lot lately. Ella made a mental note to ask George about him.

She darted her gaze across the bedroom wall, as if searching for wisdom in the monks' brain maps.

Jady broke the silence. "Are you coming home this weekend?" Her voice sounded so small.

"Yes, definitely. I can't wait to see you. We'll shop King's Road on Saturday and get our nails done."

She almost asked Jady if she wanted to spend the night at her flat again but held herself back, knowing Jady would refuse.

"Uh, okay. So, what's Bhutan like anyway?" She pronounced the name as if it were a trendy nightclub.

"It's beautiful. Very remote. Feels like another planet compared to London."

"Maybe I can come there."

"It's quite a long way, love. And school starts again next week."

Jady titled her head down.

Ella only saw the top of the hat now, and it made her wonder why she'd be wearing it inside at all.

"Jady, I can't see you, love. Can you take off your hat?"

Jady jerked her head up, eyes wide now. "Huh?" She glanced around and then back down. "No. I have to go."

What, Ella wondered, was this all about?

"I just got a text from Peter. Mum, I *have* to go. I'll call you right back."

"No. Hang on. What's up with the hat? Why is it down over your eyes like that? Take it off please."

Jady rolled her head back, her mouth open in dramatic disbelief.

"Come on, I want to see you, love."

When she tugged it off, Ella spotted the eyebrow piercing immediately. It looked like a mini barbell. "What the bleeding hell is that?"

"Ugh. I knew you'd freak out."

"Jady, we never talked about this."

"Cause you would've said no."

"Of course I would have said no." Ella heard Becca's laugh in the background. "Does your father know about this?"

"No, he's still traveling. It's no big deal, Mum."

"It is a big deal. And I want you to take it out, right away."

"No. Why? Becca's mum's fine with it."

"Well, I'm your mum, and I'm not."

Jady scoffed. "I'll talk to dad."

The knot in Ella's stomach tightened. "Look, I'm very disappointed that you just went ahead and did this."

"I know, I know. I need to go now."

"Alright, but that's coming out."

Jady's eyes moved around her screen, as if looking for a button to click and then the call ended.

First the tattoo and now a piercing, Ella thought. All because her friend had suggested it. Jady's words replayed in her mind "it was Becca's idea anyway." Her daughter didn't think for herself. And she looked awful, as though she hadn't slept in days.

She had to talk to George, make sure they were on the same page about this.

###

Jon blinked his eyes open from deep meditation, startled by the knock on his cabin door. His room service had arrived.

He signed for his lunch and thanked the short, smiling woman who'd delivered his tray. An envelope leaned on his glass of juice, the note inside a message from Neema asking him to come to the monastery at sunset. Relieved, he thought how he could get away from the Person8'ers.

The next moment, he got a text from Lex informing him that he had the afternoon off because she had to record the waterfall to use as background audio for the app. In the space of one minute, it had all worked out for Jon.

He soon found himself running along the ridge above the resort, weaving between the pines, so happy to be outdoors. He felt an added thrill from being off trail, risking unknown terrain. He pictured what he'd seen from high above yesterday, knowing that if he kept along the crest, he'd eventually meet the trail to Tiger's Nest. But as he came over a minor summit, the ridgeline forked, a split he hadn't noticed when he looked from above the day before.

The monastery was to his right, so he headed in that direction. After about a mile, the terrain peaked and then sloped steeply down to the edge of a sheer cliff. If Jon lost his footing, the slick pine needles would make it nearly impossible for him to avoid sailing over the edge. He skidded to a stop and took gentle steps backwards, leaning into the slope.

Tiger's Nest loomed ahead across the valley, but he'd have to double back to the fork to get there. The sun hung low over distant peaks, and the breeze chilled him. Jon scanned the hillside to his left for the trail, but the forest was too thick to see through. Even with his new sense of calm composure, Jon's mind raced. If he got lost, he thought, he'd miss his meeting with Neema.

He turned back the way he'd come. And as he walked, wondered why he felt so tired, if he was coming down with something. Normally, he could trail run for hours.

Back at the fork, he followed the other ridgeline that headed up and away from the monastery. This route soon flattened, and he found himself hiking aimlessly through a dense forest, hoping to stumble across the elbow of the narrow trail.

He might have already passed it, he thought, and adrenaline jitters crept down his arms. He should have taken the damn path from the Nalu Bar down to the Tiger's Nest parking lot.

Hands on his hips, deciding whether he should circle back to the resort, he spotted movement through the trees, fifty yards ahead. Dark maroon robes. Monks. He loped to catch them, almost laughing with relief and came onto the steep, dusty trail behind four men.

If they were surprised to have a lone foreigner emerge from the forest and follow them, they didn't show it.

Jon's gaze locked on the brown calves in front of him, the monk's sandals making a steady thap, thap, thap sound that put him back into the happy trance he'd felt earlier with Ella. He replayed his meeting with her, remembering those brilliant eyes and that sensual smile.

Stop. The left side of his brain had prepared a well-reasoned argument against this type of daydreaming. First things first, his brain reminded him. Figure out how to block the madness. Anything with Ella right now would turn into that vicious cycle of worry, or worse.

His right-brain conceded, offering the dramatic analogy that they'd end up like two suns colliding, so intense that they'd collapse into a black hole. In return, his left-brain murmured that it was a moot point. That she probably thought he was rude and awkward anyway.

Jon had a close, if sometimes strained relationship with his th[illegible] He recognized a difference in his thinking this afternoon. [illegible] was running at full speed, clear and sharp, but it also felt wide open. And even with the whistling tone and headache, he easily brought himself to be truly in the moment, almost transcendent.

The thapping sandals droned on, hypnotizing him. Suddenly, a laughing Bhutanese child flashed in and out of his mind's eye. The image was vivid and real. He stopped on the path. It had felt like a spontaneous memory, bringing visuals, sounds, and even a powerful loving feeling. But how? he wondered. He'd never seen that child before.

The monks turned a corner and he hurried to catch up.

Eventually, they came to a small structure and the monks took turns spinning a prayer wheel, gathering good karma and purifying bad karma. Pilgrims of all ages rested on cement benches and Jon sat among them next to a young Bhutanese man.

Jon lifted his face to the sun and a fleeting sense of lining up a target in an archery contest sprang to mind. He even felt the nervous competitive energy and, perhaps because his eyes were closed, this vision was even more vivid than the last.

He opened his eyes, shook his head in confusion and searched the faces around him, trying to guess who'd thought about archery. At the same time, he felt very disturbed at what his search implied—that he was hearing thoughts from those around him.

The gathering of gentle pilgrims now felt claustrophobic. He wandered back to wait at the trail, calming himself with deep breaths. A guide leading a mule paused next to him, waiting for his turn at the prayer wheel.

Jon nodded hello to the man and then closed his eyes to avoid further interaction. His mind filled with the sense of cutting open a green betel nut and eating it. He even felt the deep longing of an addict. Then the burst of knowing ended as quickly as it had come.

The monks rose, and Jon followed silently, wondering what on earth was happening to him. These intrusive little scraps of thought were like what he heard before sleep, he realized, but much richer, much stronger.

After more climbing and more baffling mental experiences, he raised his head to find that they'd arrived at the promontory where he'd sat the evening before. Jon and the monks proceeded onward, without pausing to admire the view and ventured onto the treacherous ledge where he'd seen the young family earlier. He kept his eyes on the ledge, hoping he wouldn't have a bizarre vision and become disoriented.

A slick footbridge crossed the base of the thundering waterfall. Thick moss blanketed the rocks and thousands of prayer flags flapped over his head on dozens of crisscrossing lines. Pilgrims crowded the way and Jon squeezed his way past. He came off the bridge and climbed up steep steps hewn out of the rock.

These final seven hundred steps made his thighs burn, and he remembered being carried here as a boy. He stole glances up to the maroon and gold ornamentation and the sheer walls of the monastery, pink from the sunset. The structure towered like a fortress through low-hanging clouds.

He felt like he was ascending to heaven.

# # #

Ella needed a drink. George hadn't reacted to news of Jady's barbell as strongly as he should have. To escape her frustration and worry, she'd spent hours analyzing Jon's astounding EEG reports while listening to the new binaural beat recording of Jon.

She slipped her headphones into her backpack and turned left out of her front door, toward the Nalu bar steps. She passed Lex's cabin, grateful not to catch even a glimpse of her. Lex had become increasingly hostile. Seeing Jeffrey's cabin up ahead, she considered asking him if he wanted to join her.

Just as she was deciding, Lex came out Jeffrey's door, slamming it behind her and stomping up to the main path, her thigh holsters swinging wildly. Ella couldn't help thinking how comical she looked.

Lex came up onto the path and blocked Ella's way, her hands on her hips.

Ella was not in the mood to be bullied.

"Where the fuck do you think you're going?" Lex said, glaring.

The best thing to do, Ella decided, was to ignore her and just go around. The hill sloped steeply up on her right, so she stepped down to the left. Lex shoved her shoulder as she passed. Ella fell backward down the hill, landing hard on the pine needles. She continued to tumble down the slope until colliding against a tree.

Stunned, she struggled to comprehend what had just happened. She'd never been physically attacked in her life, and it almost didn't seem real. She got to her feet, brushed herself off and, thankfully, didn't feel any major injuries. She knew the right call was to go down the hill and have dinner at the Beyul restaurant. But when she looked up and saw Lex smirking, her pride swelled, and she found herself scrambling back up.

"What the hell is wrong with you?" Ella said, crawling back onto the path, her heart pounding.

"I asked you a simple question. Where do you think you're going?"

"I'm going up to the bar."

"Oh really," Lex said, deadpan. "Well then, go right ahead." She stepped aside, blocking the steps down to Venn's cabin, and waving her arm like a militant game show hostess.

Ella slipped by, on the uphill side this time, and started climbing the stairs.

Lex followed, her boots heavy and close behind.

"Nice ass," Lex said.

Before Ella could process the remark, a sharp sting hit her backside, and she felt as if a giant had grabbed hold of her spine and was shaking her like a doll. She crumpled to the steps, the pain filling every part of her, drowning out any thought other than a vague awareness of her own convulsing.

After an agonizing five seconds, she started to come back to her senses. Now, almost worse than her pain was her feeling of powerlessness. She sat up and noticed she was crying.

Lex was laughing, deep from her belly at the bottom of the stairs.

Ella's first real thought was that she had to report this. Lex had to be arrested. She couldn't just go around tasering people.

"Well, go on," Lex shouted, nodding up the stairs.

Heading down was not an option. Ella rose and stumbled up the rest of the way. At the top, her heart thumping out of her chest, she took a moment to steady herself before moving onto the terrace.

The sunset gave the white cushions and stone floor a warm pink glow. A dark skinned family of four, wearing brightly colored robes ate an early dinner around the fire pit, the mother cutting something on her son's plate. A warm, gusty breeze swirled smoke from the fire and brought the hint of curry and cardamom from their stew.

After the trauma on the stairs, she felt almost as if she were dreaming. She sat on a cushioned stool at the small, empty bar and took in the spectacular view of snow-covered peaks. Rays of the late sun beamed through breaks in the heavy, luminous clouds, creating patches of vibrant green that inched across the darkening pine valley.

The gray-haired bartender seemed delighted to have her there, and he easily talked her into having a Nalu-Ara, the house special drink made with local rice wine, gin, lemon juice and syrup.

The image of Lex smiling from the bottom of the stairs came to mind. She'd gotten real pleasure from inflicting pain, Ella realized. She was a psychopath.

The drink arrived, tasting like a sweet, cold lemonade, and she held herself back from finishing it in one go. She thought back to how submissive she'd been with Lex all week and how it had made Lex bolder. Ella knew she had to tell Jeffrey, the resort manager, and the police, but not right now, she decided. Lex was probably still lurking around down there or watching from her cabin window.

Ella just needed to escape, and Jon's new binaural beat recording was the best distraction she could think of. She pulled on her headphones, closed her eyes, and let Jon's brainwaves hammer her ears relentlessly. Moving only to sip her drink, she took no notice of the other guests that came and went and ignored the spicy red and green chiles she ordered.

She'd used entrainment to rewire her brain over the past few years, moving from alpha waves that calmed her, to theta waves that gave her the feeling of being on the edge of sleep. This track was different—it consumed her.

She sighed loudly and lost herself in the steady hum.

# # #

Jon met a young monk at the gate. His shaved head, beaming smile, and maroon robe made him seem identical to Jon's climbing companions.

"I am Sonam. Welcome. Please remove your shoes and put your phone in here." He held out a copper bowl.

Jon took off his trail running shoes and explained that he didn't have his phone with him.

"And you will need this," Sonam said, handing over a cloth maroon jacket that looked hand-washed a thousand times.

Still sweating from his hike, Jon tied it around his waist and followed the monk inside. Yak butter lamps flickered a warm ethereal glow and heady sandalwood incense filled the air.

Sonam bowed as he passed a table crowded with Buddhist icons and heaped with offerings of money and food.

Jon bowed as well, patted his empty pockets, and followed Sonam to a stone stairway. His calves threatened to seize as they wound up, and he took deliberate, flat-footed steps.

At the top of the stairs, Sonam turned to face him in front of a large, intricately engraved door. "First we bring Buddha's power into your body." He opened the door onto a large hall, packed with meditating monks. Like statues, they sat upright in perfect rows facing an elder monk, chanting on the far side of the room. Sonam wove soundlessly to the front and sat cross-legged.

Jon trailed behind, navigating his way carefully. He didn't trust his weary legs for balance and was glad once he'd settled next to Sonam.

The young monk closed his eyes, his shoulders melted, and his chin rose a fraction. It was as though he were instantly lost in a trance. As though he'd been longing to return here.

Jon's mind continued its odd racing calmness. He was too tall, had too much hair, no robe and no idea what exactly to do, but he was perfectly okay with it. He glanced around the rows of calm faces and shaved heads, and then tried to identify the deities in the frescoes covering the walls. Looking through the large open windows, to threads of cloud weaving between mountain peaks, felt like looking out of an airplane. He wondered if this was the room where he'd first learned aikido as a boy. He let himself become more in sync with the gentle rhythm of the monastery and the strangeness of his past twenty-four hours dissolved into a sense of peace.

The elder monk paused in his chant. He turned to Jon and smiled, as though he knew him. He gestured at the copper bowl between them for Jon to make a cup with his hands, bring it to his lips and then splash it onto the crown of his head.

The water looked like it had been laced with saffron and as Jon poured it over his head, it ran cold down his nose and behind his right ear.

The monk resumed his chanting and, soon after, Sonam rose.

Jon followed him out. The sky had grown a darker shade of red. They climbed stairs carved into the mountain. He looked up to see a smaller temple, a solid structure merging directly into the cliff. He thought how there was something familiar about it, something that made him uneasy.

Sonam paused at the top. The step was wider in front of the double doors.

"This temple protects the cave where Guru Rinpoche meditated for three years. The door that seals the cave opens only once a year in a special ceremony. A blessing of compassion." He put his palms together in front of his face, closed his eyes, and bowed.

Jon mimicked the gesture and suddenly felt dizzy, as if he were slightly drunk. He lost his balance and almost tumbled down the steep steps they'd just come up. Sonam caught his arm, and the feeling passed. At what point, Jon considered, should he stop blaming his odd behavior on the altitude or some kind of bug?

The inside of this temple felt considerably cooler than the last, and as the front door closed behind them with a thud, Jon was momentarily lost in complete darkness. His eyes adjusted to see thin lines of light squeezing through thick shutters and two candles burning on the far side of the room. He put on his maroon jacket and shadowed Sonam toward the candles.

A ghostly figure sat guarding a massive, ornate wooden door. Neema.

She wore her usual orange shirt and maroon robe, her right arm and shaved head completely bare, a silk wrap the only accommodation to the chill.

Sonam bowed then scurried back out to the sunset.

Neema stared far into the distance, motionless, as if posing for a fresco of her own.

Jon looked to the ancient door behind her, remembering how as a child the idea of pitch-blackness on the other side had terrified him. Not wanting to bother her, he sat cross-legged on a pillow direct line of sight, fumbling and fidgeting to point his feet inward in the respectful position.

As before, the whistling in his head seemed louder in the complete silence, but it also felt nice to sit. By his usual trail running standards, the hike up here should have been easy, even considering the altitude, yet now he fought the urge to lie down.

Neema's face fluttered in the candlelight.

He imagined her exploring the depths of the deep cave behind her, communing with centuries-dead prophets. Then he closed his eyes, took a few deep, relaxed breaths, and felt his mind shift as he went inward. His trance deepened and as on the hike, memory-like thoughts appeared. These were more familiar yet still seemed to come from outside him. He saw his mother and then himself as a young boy hanging robes on a line. Then himself again at the same young age, posing and controlled, in the aikido ready position.

Jon opened his eyes, realizing that the strange, foreign thoughts emerged every time he went inward, like rocks surfacing in a low tide. At least these last images were more familiar. Maybe they were a memory. But, he wondered, how could he see himself in a memory?

A cold breath came from under the cave door, as if from the very mouth of the Himalayas, and he pulled his jacket around him.

Neema turned, her eyes boring into him and then softening as she gradually saw him.

"Welcome back, Jon," she said, her voice barely above a whisper, sounding as though she hadn't spoken in days.

"Thank you for seeing me. It's amazing to be here again."

She remained still, comfortable in the silence.

"I met a woman, here in Bhutan," Jon said, immediately confused why he'd chosen to talk about Ella first. "There's something unusual between us."

Neema smiled, her face radiant in the soft glow of the candles. "That's wonderful."

"It might be, but I'm not sure what to think at this point, what to do."

"Just be present with her. Once your mind is out of the way, your heart will open."

Sometimes Neema sounded like a self-help book, Jon thought.

"No, I mean, she's distracting."

"Distracting you from what?"

"What I came here to do."

"Ah, the phone app you mentioned in your letter," Neema said, the corner of her mouth turning up.

"Ha, no. I need more of a boundary, remember? Like we said in California?"

"I spoke of your gift. And how it makes you what you are."

Which is lonely, Jon thought. "Well, if it is a gift, could you help me learn how to control it?"

"Control?" She narrowed her eyes, as if offended.

"Manage?"

She tilted her head as if to say that he was getting closer to the correct word.

After a few moments of her holding his gaze, he felt a warm, open feeling spread across his upper body.

"That's right," Neema said. "Allow. Be open. Pain comes from resisting." She tapped her forehead with her index finger. "Let in what you feel and then let it go. See what remains."

What if it's too much, he wanted to ask. What if it makes me crazy? "Easy for you maybe," he said.

"Shhh, I'm nothing special." Neema leaned in with a candid grin. "When I was young, some said I was dakini, so I traveled to meet the Dalai Lama. People I stay with sometimes say to me, 'Why rely on us? Why do you have to eat the food and take shelter here? Why don't you simply pull the sun down here?' And so on. Some said I was mad. I still don't know." She laughed.

"You're not mad, Neema."

With almost comical timing, her smile faded, and her gaze drifted and deepened as though she'd heard something, seen something in the dark chamber.

Again unsure what to do, Jon figured he might as well go inward as well, and he quickly slid into a deep, floating state. His thoughts remained on Neema and he was soon given unintelligible pieces of what seemed like profound insights. Bizarre visions of what looked like bright whirling balls of yarn flashed into his mind. He opened his eyes after what might have been five seconds or five minutes.

Neema sat unchanged.

He cleared his throat. "Thank you. I'll meditate on what you've told me." Jon rose and the dizzy, drunken feeling returned. He was definitely coming down with something.

She whispered, "We can change. Transform ourselves. Go deep inside. Don't be afraid. Be clear about what you want."

"Okay."

Neema let out a long breath, still coming out of her latest trance.

He realized he hadn't asked her about the voice. "Remember the voice I heard when we fought?"

"Yes," Neema said. "She spoke out of the field, where your movements came from during the fight."

"It *was* a female voice." Jon remembered how the voice had felt ageless, personal and impersonal, both nearby and from the edge of the universe. "Who is she?"

"I can only guess. Maybe Nairatmya, a female Buddha known as the Selfless One. Or maybe—" Neema paused and looked down to her lap, a string of beads clicking in her hands, as if deciding to speak further. "Or maybe you heard Dharmakāya, the body of reality itself. What's important is that you heard what is expected of you. You should let it be your guide."

Jon nodded, but wondered how "this is not Jon," could possibly be an expectation, or even helpful. A gust of wind hissed at the shutters, bringing him back to where he stood, back to his predicament. "I'll be done with this project in a few days. Could I come stay with you here? Learn to manage my gift?"

Neema picked up a coil of red string from the low table in front of her and used a tiny blade to cut off about seven inches. She motioned for Jon's left arm.

Kneeling in front of her, he remembered from his boyhood that monks used these as a protection and blessing, a moral guidepost.

She tied the cord around his wrist. "Remember to allow. To be open." Her warm hands held his. "You have a different path. You will grow your consciousness by how you choose to respond to the experiences given to you. I know you'll choose well."

They sat in silence, staring into each other's eyes for a long moment and, unlike the eye gazing sessions with his clients, Jon felt as if he were the one being recharged and vitalized. Even the insane whistling tone became bearable. He thought to ask her about it, but again Neema shifted her gaze, as if she'd heard a voice of her own, from somewhere high in the mountains.

She started to tremble and twitch, her dark eyes staring miles in the distance, like windows onto a nonhuman consciousness.

He knew he was witnessing her 'self' disappearing within an experience of such depth and subtlety that any scientific explanation Ella could develop for it would fall short. Rather than interrupt her, he rose and let himself out, to a sky now as dark as the chamber.

He'd ask Ella about the whistling in his head tomorrow.

###

Ella felt an itch, like an odd shudder, behind her right ear. She took off the headphones and realized she'd been listening to Jon's new track for more than an hour. Stretching her neck, she searched the deep black sky for any sign of the moon or stars through the thick clouds. Only faint specks of light came from Tiger's Nest on the opposite side of the valley.

The Nalu-Ara drinks were going down fast, and Ella waved her finger to order a fourth. She tapped her phone screen to turn off the binaural beat recording and, seeing the file name, was reminded that it was Jon's brain she was listening to and copying onto her own. She thought that while he had a remarkable brain, he also had issues. How did he function with that level of sensitivity? she wondered.

The bartender served her a fresh drink with a shy, almost blushing smile.

She thanked him, and when she returned the smile, he scooted back to his post by the beer taps. She pulled out a fresh straw from her drink to play with. Maybe, she thought, if she scanned herself every few hours to track the effect, she could get a boost in her brainpower but not get Jon's full openness. At worst, she might get some of his awkwardness from his high-beta brainwaves and quiet calmness from his low-gamma.

Unconsciously folding the straw into small sections, she thought that perhaps Jon seemed aloof and awkward because he wasn't interested in her. And so what? she thought. How did she feel about him? She admitted that she'd never felt an instant connection like this before. But he was an odd bird, so different than most men. So different than Jeffrey.

Over the past week at the isolated resort, Jeffrey had proved to be her best option for company. Lex threatened her and Oliver ignored her. Most of the other guests kept to themselves. So even though Jeffrey seemed far too impressed with himself, Ella found it hard to refuse his regular invitations to share a meal or go on a hike. As the week wore on, she became fascinated by his powerful mind.

She gulped at her drink.

Feeling very alone, she picked up her phone to check for texts. Jady hadn't sent a text, nor had she called Ella's cabin as she had promised. To be fair, Ella thought, she hadn't called Jady back either. She also hadn't imparted any wisdom on their calls, just absent pauses and letting herself be cut off. What kind of mother understood less about parenting with every year?

She had to be stronger.

A warm hand brushed her back. She turned to see Venn taking the stool next to her.

"Oh, hi Jeffrey."

"What are we drinking?" he said.

"Nalu-Aras. They're delicious, but dangerous."

"Perfect." He snapped his fingers to the bartender, as if competing for attention in a crowded New York club. "Another round." He turned to face her, one of his loafers on her stool's footrest.

"Ella Sandström, outstanding job. I've been listening to the Gunnarson recording. This is going to be huge, and I couldn't have done it without you."

Venn went on to describe his social media plan supporting the launch, using words like crafty and bold.

A chilly breeze swept up from the valley and Ella shivered. She was about to mention Lex's attack, when Venn fitted his silk blazer onto her shoulders, wrapping her in a sharp and woody cologne.

The bartender brought their drinks and apologized that it was nine p.m. and almost time to close.

Venn ignored the man and raised his glass. "To Tuning In."

Ella drank with a vague sense of dread; the alcohol had dulled her senses enough to overlook that they were toasting a scam with her name all over it. Her deal with Venn meant that in return for him paying for the MRI truck and her cabin at the resort, she had to not only create the binaural tracks of Jon but also to participate in promoting the app.

She blinked to try and clear her head.

As if sensing her concern, Venn took on a more reflective tone. "I like it here. It's been good to get away."

Again, Ella was about to bring up Lex's attack but, as usual, he quickly continued talking.

"Gives you some perspective, you know? Like, I've always put my business first. My dad wasn't around much but I remember him saying that money's the best way to keep score. Well, I'm not sure if he's right anymore. You see, this past week with you has opened my eyes. I want to create things that make a difference, that help people."

Ella wished there were actually such a thing as telepathy. He seemed sincere, but how much of this was just a script to get her into bed?

"Like you do," he said, and took her hand. His sharp gray eyes darted, as if gauging the situation. He caught her glance, gave a bright white smile and winked.

Oh my God, she thought, did he really just wink at me?

But the wink worked because it activated the reward system of Ella's brain. George Clooney, she thought, that's who he looks like. She studied his forearm muscles, flexing like thick cords.

"How can such a beautiful girl be such a smart scientist?"

Normally, this was a conversation ender, but Ella blushed instead. She wasn't really listening anymore as her frontal cortex, the region of her brain essential to judgment, had effectively shut down. Years ago, her professor had described this process as nature purposefully suspending rational judgment in the interest of higher, reproductive purposes.

She felt a different kind of pulsing now and a warm, wet tingling. She shifted her hips on the cushion. Her breathing deepened and she craved to be touched, to be filled.

Venn finished his drink, took hold of her wrist. "You're freezing. Come with me."

Ella was more than a little unsteady, but Venn's strong arms guided her off the stool and down steps that seemed to wobble beneath her feet.

His firm hand on her hip urged her into his cabin. Then he shut the door and kissed her, his weight pushing her into the wall.

More than anything, she felt his will, his strength—the strength she needed for herself.

# # #

Jon wished Neema didn't talk in riddles. He replayed her advice as he followed the long path back to the resort. She'd told him to be even more open and then let go whatever he took in. As if it were so easy.

Fireflies blinked around him in the dark valley floor. A few lit up at the same time. Then more. All at once hundreds of the little bugs flashed together as one, like a slow strobe light. He'd heard about this phenomenon, this synchronization without any apparent means of communication. Being in the middle of it was otherworldly.

He finally reached the Tiger's Nest parking lot—he hadn't wanted to chance the tricky shortcut in the dark—and started up the trail leading back up to the resort. As he fell into a steady climbing rhythm, the odd visions began flashing in his mind again. This time, the visions were associated with the resort: the fire pit at the Nalu Bar, the zig-zag steps, and then a cabin.

Continuing his climb, and fascinated to see what would come next, he suddenly had the sense of being in bed, with a naked man moving over him in dim light. Powerful feelings of desire came with these thoughts and Jon found himself becoming deeply aroused.

Whoa.

As before, the visions ended as quickly as they'd arrived, leaving him more confused than ever. For his entire life, he'd been figuring out where his feelings came from. Many women, including Danielle and Lex had made him feel out of control down there many times before. Like those times, this sudden arousal felt foreign. After all, he was alone in a Bhutanese forest, thinking about Neema's advice. Plus, he'd never wanted a man like that.

The path opened onto the resort's empty hilltop bar. The gray-haired bartender waved and apologized that he'd just closed up for the night.

Jon crossed the patio and headed down the stairs, shaking his shoulders and arms to get the quivers out, and trying to ignore what was happening in his pants. Thinking how he'd need to add "spontaneous erection" to his curious list of sensations. How he was losing his mind.

Neema had basically refused to help him control his condition, which was the whole reason he came here. She'd only said something about allowing himself to go deep inside and to grow by how he responded to experiences.

Thankfully, tomorrow he could ask one of the top neuroscientists in the world.

Thursday, October 18

Ella's hangover was splitting her head apart. Which made it impossible to stay horizontal in Jeffrey's bed any longer. She dressed without waking him and crept through the main room, squinting against the rays of sun blasting through the tall windows. Then she trotted along the path to her cabin, carrying her sneakers, the pine needles sharp on her bare feet.

Lex called out from her doorstep. She wore a maroon bathrobe, as if heading to the spa.

Ella broke into a run. She cut the corner to the path leading down to her cabin and luckily found her card key in the first pocket she checked. She shut the door before Lex appeared, then called Jeffrey and finally told him what had happened the day before.

An hour later, she sipped her second coffee near the smoky Nalu Bar firepit, her head still pounding, cursing the bashful bartender and his evil drinks from the night before.

Gautam Kumar, the cameraman from Mumbai, scurried about the hilltop searching for the best view of Tiger's Nest as a backdrop.

Lex dropped the script for the promotional video in her lap without a word. It seemed Jeffrey had reprimanded her because her holsters were empty.

Ella dreaded the day on multiple levels. Being around Lex, completely hungover, topped the list. A close second was the fact that this meditation app, already something a prominent scientist like herself shouldn't be associated with, had suddenly turned into a bloody telepathy app. Apparently, it had been all along, and they'd been lying to her. The promotional video alone would crush her credibility.

She squinted at the script where Jeffrey had scrawled "Stretch the truth" across the top. Ugh.

Ella knew she really had no choice given the terms of her contract with Venn. What had seemed like incredible luck a few weeks ago, had become an ordeal.

She retreated into her headphones, hoping that somehow the steady hum of Jon's binaural beat track would help her hangover, or at least take her mind off it.

A few minutes later, Jon came up the stairs on the far side of the patio wearing khaki shorts and a faded black t-shirt which, she noticed, fell on him quite nicely. Last night must have unlocked something, she thought. She'd been celibate since her divorce two years ago, focusing on her research as usual. Now, after having drunken sex with a morally vacant man, she eyed Jon as if he were her next conquest.

He had that rugged Nordic thing going for sure, she thought, nibbling her fingernail. Tall with broad shoulders and chest, his rosy skin and messy reddish-brown hair made him look like a real-life Viking. The only thing missing was the beard.

He kept his gaze on the path, each step deliberate, as though unsure of his footing.

Now that she knew his baseline brain state, frequencies usually associated with a mix of complex thought and transcendence, she understood why he might walk like that. While she appreciated his looks, she realized it was his unique mind that made him so attractive to her.

She was about to call him over when Lex intercepted him. She touched his forearm and leaned in close. After a minute, she nodded in Ella's direction and Jon glanced up, with what might have been a look of surprise, almost as if Lex had just told him about her walk of shame this morning. As if they were back in college.

Lex went off to corral Gautam, and Jon turned away to put his face to the sun.

Not very social, Ella thought and then admitted she wasn't being very social either. She took off her headphones, grabbed a breakfast bar from her bag, and walked over to him, thinking how silly she must look in the scrubs Jeffrey made her wear.

"Brilliant morning, huh?" she said.

Jon turned and smiled.

He had a nice smile too, Ella thought.

"Brilliant," he said. "Just catching some sun before it disappears again."

"Want one of these?" Ella said, holding out a bar. "They're pretty good."

"No thanks, I did the smoked bacon at Beyul."

"Okay. Uh, we need to talk. Your transcendent state is forty-two hertz. That's high gamma."

Jon shrugged, clearly not understanding how dramatic this was, how this would be another published study.

"How many hours a day do you meditate?"

"I don't really meditate. I just kinda sit on my porch a lot."

"The monks I've recorded at gamma meditate for at least four hours a day. For decades."

Jon pushed out his lower lip.

Ella thought how Jon had nice lips too, but in the brief time she'd stood next to him, her headache had become a powerful migraine.

Lex swooped in. "Hey, we need to get started before it rains."

Ninety minutes into their session, Gautam said, "Let's try that again," for what had to be the tenth time, deleting yet another failed scene.

Jon brushed sweaty hair from his forehead and Ella caught a tangy sharpness wafting up from his shirt when he moved his arm. He seemed unable to focus on his lines and Ella began to wonder if he was on the spectrum, mildly autistic. The next take didn't go any better. Jon lost his place and turned to her, a confused look on his face, as if she'd asked him a question.

Gautam cut the take and suggested a break for lunch.

Thankfully, Lex had disappeared back down the hill, but Ella still couldn't eat with her hangover, or whatever it was, and found herself inexplicably drawn back to Jon's track. He'd gone off to sit on a rock so she put her headphones on. When she tapped the screen to start the audio, she saw a text from Jeffrey.

"Ready for round two."

How romantic, she thought, and turned the phone over. She wished she could ignore him like that when they were together in person. Jeffrey had this charm, this power, this *something.* He reminded her of Johan Karlsson, her charismatic high school boyfriend who'd had her in the palm of his hand. If Jeffrey showed up here, she knew she may just go back to his cabin, headache and all.

I must get out of here, she thought. She picked up her phone to see what time she needed to leave for the airport the next day. Looking at her screen made her nauseous, so instead she bent over and rubbed that pesky itch behind her right ear again.

Jon's feet appeared in front of her.

She peeled off the headphones.

"Hey there," he said, hands in his pockets. "You okay?"

"I'll live. Unless my head explodes."

He smiled, pointed to the headphones in her hand. "Listening to my brain?"

"Yeah. I seem to be addicted to it, even though it's like a slow drill boring into my skull."

"Welcome to my world."

She stood, feeling unsteady.

Jon opened his palms.

For a moment, she prepared herself to be hugged.

"Sorry if I've been rude," he said.

Ella nodded vaguely, then surprised herself by giving him a quick hug. "Not at all."

He tensed and brought his hand to his head.

"You have a headache too?" she said.

"Brutal. Probably the altitude. I also have this high-pitched tone whistling in my head. It started yesterday. I was kind of getting used to it but right now it's deafening."

"A tone? In only your right ear? or both ears?"

"My right, I guess. I don't know." He shook his head slowly from side to side. "It's not in my ear, it's like it's inside my brain. What do you think it is?"

"Well, it can't be in your brain, because there are no sensory nerves in the brain itself. It's probably some damage in your ear that's giving you Tinnitus. Is your hearing okay?"

Jon nodded, wincing.

"Any other symptoms?"

"Yeah, plenty. I had a dizzy spell last night." He shifted his gaze over her shoulder, looking behind her. "Like vertigo."

Ella turned, following his line of sight to Tigers Nest across the valley. That place had a way of holding your attention. She brought her mind back to diagnosing. Meniere's disease would explain both his vertigo and the Tinnitus, but she knew better than to speculate out loud, especially since the causes of the disease were unknown and there was no known cure.

"You should have it fully checked out when you get home. And your headache, where is it?"

"It's back here." He tapped behind his right ear.

What a coincidence, Ella thought. Her pain centered in the same place.

He stared at her for a moment, his eyes such a bright blue that they seemed lit from within. They were lonely eyes but calm and steady. A lover's eyes that suffered, healed, and *knew*. Eyes that somehow knew of the husband and daughter she'd lost for the sake of science. For her unrelenting need to prove herself.

At some point, a fly landed on his cheek.

Ella blinked, noticing in her peripheral vision the hillside around them. She realized they'd been staring into each other's eyes for quite some time. She took a deep, easy breath, finding herself surprisingly calm, as if all the tension she'd been carrying had disappeared.

Jon continued holding her gaze in the most gentle way, making no move to brush the fly away.

Before he'd approached her, she'd had the beginnings of a crush. Now she felt as if she'd known him her whole life, as if she could trust him with her life.

Gautam called them for another try.

She squeezed Jon's hand and smiled. "We can do this."

# # #

Venn read from his laptop. "They call it, placing me in custody pending court proceedings."

"This is not good," Max Harding said, glaring from a window on Venn's screen. "An FBI search warrant means they arrest you."

Venn sat alone in his spacious cabin, fighting to stay in denial that the FBI had finally caught up with him for years of Internet fraud.

Harding looked down, reading from a printed sheet. "You will appear before a US magistrate within seventy-two hours of arrest." He turned back to Venn, purple bags under his watery eyes. "They've arrested you, Jeffrey."

"Well, here's the next sentence in the letter," Venn said. "At this initial appearance, the judge will determine whether there is probable cause to believe that the arrestee committed a crime. How could they have probable cause? We're untraceable."

"You'll find out in five days. Unless you decide to hide out in Bhutan for the rest of your life."

Not funny, Venn thought. "Yeah, shave my head, be a monk."

"That's funny," Harding said. "Now, I want my three hundred grand back."

"It's gone, wired to the media vehicles. The campaign's running."

"Then stop it. And get my money back."

Venn flushed. "I'm setting up new accounts, the revenue will be safe—"

"I don't care," Harding said, leaning in to the camera.

"Hey, I've got three hundred in this too, or more. Look, you saw the early data. We can make our investment back before I fly out on Monday."

Harding raised a meaty finger. "That money better be in my account before you land in New York."

The screen went blank.

Venn realized the FBI wasn't his only concern. He had to pay Harding back; he'd heard stories about guys who hadn't. How could he pay him back if he got arrested and had all his assets frozen? He had to front-end the media plan even more and blow this thing out in the first few days.

He picked up the hotel phone to call Lex but stopped short, remembering the hateful stare she'd given him when they'd talked about Ella earlier that morning. Lex had bragged how she'd once served time for nearly beating another woman to death, just for dirty dancing with her boyfriend.

Venn put down the receiver, telling himself to keep his distance from Lex for a while.

###

Jon shivered, wet from mist, in the shadow of the sheer stone walls at the top of the resort's waterfall. Performing in the promotional videos had been nearly impossible, with the random thought flashes coming rapid fire, visions of Indian children jumping rope, of New York subways and, strangest of all, visions of himself in the moment, which created a powerful, repeating sense of deja-vu.

The swish of the river and the rumble from the boulders below made the whistling tone in his head almost manageable. Combined, the sounds felt like a three-dimensional field of white noise. He closed his eyes and breathed into it, trying to become one with it.

He switched his attention between each sound, making one or the other seem louder, and noticed that the whistling tone stood out because of its fluctuations. Jon thought how it wouldn't be so bad if it were a steady pitch, and he focused intently on it, hoping that by sheer will he could control it and smooth it out.

Minutes passed and finally the tone held steady a moment longer than usual. He figured it was probably just a coincidence, but he zeroed in on it, holding his own pitch in his mind, as if humming a constant note over a song. Gradually, the wavering tone's peaks and valleys above and below his pitch shrank until aligning with him, coming in tune with him.

He opened his eyes in shock and it instantly wandered again. For the next hour, Jon wrestled with the whistle in his head. He began taming it, even guiding it up and down himself.

Encouraged but exhausted, he let the tone go back to its mad wavering and leaned back on the wet stone. It had the same comforting, earthy scent as after a heavy rain back in Northern California. Pieces of his life from back home came to him: his cottage, his bike, his porch. He tried reassuring himself that a solid, safe reality awaited his return.

But a more complete picture took shape: his failure in aikido, his failure as a healer, and his failure to manage his empath condition. With the benefit of distance, he saw that even his minimalist life had unraveled. Two weeks ago, he'd heard that weird voice and had lost the fight against Neema. Which had cost him the job at the dojo. Then he'd been with Danielle, which had made him quit his healing practice. And he'd thought *that* had been a tough week.

He decided it was time to find Ella and ask her about the whistling, and while he was at it, about disconnecting. He left the patio, took the narrow path around the cliff and came in front of Venn's cabin. Out of the corner of his eye, he saw movement inside. As he turned his head to look, he nearly bumped into Ella coming around a bend in the other direction.

"Sorry," he said, taking a step back.

"No, that's fine." She looked to his wet hair and shoulders and gestured to Venn's cabin. "Were you in the hot tub?"

"The waterfall," he said.

"Oh. You know you're not supposed to go in it."

"Ha, yeah, what was I thinking?" Jon thought how beautiful she was. Not just her looks, but her passion to answer life's biggest questions.

Ella glanced to the cabin and then back to him.

Their eyes locked. The wind whooshed the pines above them.

Say something, Jon thought. "Okay, well, you going in?" That was lame.

"Uh, yeah. He wanted to wrap up before I leave tomorrow."

Jon's heart beat wildly, as if knowing what he was going to do before his conscious brain did.

"Do you have a sec?"

Ella blinked, glanced away.

He could hardly breathe. What did he think he was doing? With all the sophistication of a high schooler, he heard himself say, "I know it's only been a couple days, but I feel something with you. I mean, even more than I usually do."

Ella cocked her head.

"You know, with my gift? But with you, there's something else."

"I know."

Her confirmation gave Jon enough courage to lean in and kiss her. His only thought was how good it felt. Then he noticed that the whistling tone had gone silent. Startled by its sudden absence, he drew back and froze.

Ella leaned in and kissed him back.

Spellbound, Jon reeled in the warm softness of her lips, his exhilaration, his doubt, heightened like never before. He tasted the peach she must have just eaten and then, oddly, as if from Ella's perspective, he felt the bristly stubble of his own chin. He literally lost himself in the kiss.

She pulled away, grinning.

Jon grinned too, giddy. The conceptual idea to *kiss him again* flashed in his mind.

Ella put her hands to the back of his head and kissed him deeply, this time her tongue finding his.

Something rattled Jon in that moment. He'd heard Ella's thought process to kiss him. He knew it was her because in addition to the obvious timing, her mental tone of voice was somehow as recognizable as her speaking voice.

This cannot be happening.

Unlike the quick visions he'd been having lately, this was a steady feed of confusing noise and raw ideas. It was unfiltered, untranslated into words and sentences, and mixed in with feelings and sensations. He was hearing everything in her mind, every fleeting notion, which made this the kiss of his life but also distracted him from it.

Ella spoke, her lips brushing his. "We shouldn't be …" She kissed him again. "Doing this here." She pulled away and glanced to Venn's cabin, then turned and, holding Jon's hand, led him back the way she'd come.

Jon found he could still hear himself think if he focused on it. The left side of his brain asked what the heck he was doing kissing Ella and reminded him this was not the plan at all.

Despite his own warnings, he stayed with her, and soon realized that even with all information he was receiving—or perhaps because it was too much—he only got a rough sense of what was on her mind. He couldn't keep up with her lightning-fast mental leaps as she raced with indecision, bouncing back and forth between desire and her sense of propriety in a more intuitive than rational way.

He only caught quick, vague notions, like fleeting glimpses, about this being their last day, about whether to hold Jon's hand and how Venn would react. Jon assumed that her thoughts about Venn related to her feeling bad about missing her meeting.

They entered her cabin and she turned toward the bedroom, raising a finger and saying over her shoulder that she'd get him a towel for his hair.

He really didn't care about his hair.

Jon stood mute, the computer fans whirring, with a clear view of her freshly made bed through the open door. He doubted if he could even make love with all the distracting noise going on in his head.

He heard Ella recognize that they were alone and felt an impulsive thrill rush through her. Moving toward her room, he heard another vague reference to Venn. There was enough guilty feeling from her to make Jon stay in the main room.

Ella closed the bathroom door.

Jon got the sense from her that she needed a moment in private to think. Instinctively, he tried to shift his focus away from her thoughts and onto what he was experiencing.

Obviously, he wasn't hearing in the usual sense. The rare times when she slowed to form inner monologue, it felt like he was remembering her talking. Most of what came to him were incredibly fast thought forms, visions and feelings, and it was nearly impossible to follow them, to translate them into words and sentences in real time.

What the hell? He asked himself. He'd wanted Ella's help to manage his boundaries with other people, not *this.* Jon sighed, but a short sigh, the kind he'd give if he found his fridge empty. He knew he should be freaking out, but he felt surprisingly detached. In fact, beyond the noise of Ella's thoughts, Jon had a euphoric, floating feeling overall. Possibly because the whistling tone and headache had gone. Or possibly because he'd just kissed an incredible woman.

No, this was much more, he thought to himself, like transcendence.

He allowed the feeling to take him over, and in the process, he stopped trying to decipher the non-stop noise from Ella. Once he stopped trying, her thoughts came through as patterns of knowing, which Jon easily translated in his mind. He just *knew* what was on her mind.

She continued her wrangling about what to do with him.

Jon felt uncomfortable, like he was eavesdropping. He wandered to her desk to divert his attention. A note lay in the middle, "Went for a hike. Thurs 4pm. –Ella," it read.

She hadn't mentioned a hike, Jon thought. She'd said Venn wanted to wrap up their work. Had she lied? he wondered. The note to Oliver didn't mention Venn either.

He considered these questions with equanimity, as if he weren't attached to the answers. Yet he still wanted to know the answer. He tried probing her mind for a clue, but even at the higher, knowing level, he only got conceptual thoughts as they were surfacing in her mind. He couldn't dig into her memory.

She was coming out, and he heard her think that she wanted to slow things down. To talk.

Ella came into the room and walked toward the small fridge. "Want a beer?"

"Sure, thanks."

"I can't believe we're leaving tomorrow."

Jon noticed that a split-second before Ella spoke, he sometimes heard a quick, conceptual version of whatever she said. Like a pre-echo.

"Yeah, this week has flown by," he said.

They clinked their bottles together and as they drank, Jon had an odd, vague sense of himself. Not like looking in the mirror, but as if he were hyper-aware of himself.

Ella sighed. "I feel so calm when I'm with you."

Jon only stared, wanting to say that he felt transcendent with her, but he could barely hear himself think. This was harder to ignore than the whistling tone. Even with his new sense of equanimity, how could he live like this? he wondered. He'd have to be even more of a hermit.

A hint of concern narrowed her eyes and he heard her trying to figure out what he was thinking.

He had to tell her. Maybe she could help. He looked from one eye to the other. "Just say it," he told himself.

"Ella, I'm hearing your thoughts."

"What?" She backed her head away.

"Yeah, I hear what you're thinking. Right now."

"What are you talking about?" She laughed and searched his face for any sign that he was joking.

Jon nodded. He felt a mix of disappointment and fear rising in her. His old empath gift was still with him too. "Here, let's do a test," he said. "Think of a number."

She rolled her eyes. "Okay."

"Seven?"

"Alright, another one," she said.

"Ninety-two?"

Every time he asked her to think of something new, he was able to identify it. He correctly identified an assortment of items—her mother's cat, her car, the London Eye Ferris wheel. After conjuring up the last image, the framed picture of her daughter, Jady, at her bedside, Ella swayed a little.

Jon relived through her the sense of awe, amazement and fear of his new ability.

"I'm sorry," he said. "I didn't mean to scare you."

Ella eyed him, her hand over her mouth.

"It's totally bizarre, I know," he said.

Ella swayed again.

Jon reached out to steady her, and she pulled away.

"Have you been doing this all along?" she asked.

"No, it just started. It happened when we kissed. I've got to stop it. I can't live like this."

"Oh my God. This is really happening."

"Yes, I'm afraid so."

Ella rubbed her face and Jon heard her stunned disbelief give way to stunned excitement about the scientific breakthrough she'd been handed.

"Maybe we can see something going on in there."

"Whatever you can do."

"Here, sit."

Jon sat in the same wooden chair.

Ella absently put the towel on her desk as she woke the computers.

"We really need an fMRI. But we can do a basic map with the EEG," she said, bringing him the wire mesh cap. She saw his damp hair and reached to grab the towel. Her note to Oliver slid to the floor and landed face up, a few feet in front of her.

Ella's stream of thoughts swerved briefly from the task at hand. She considered that Venn might be curious about where she was. Once again, she had that flash of guilt. It was deeper than a professional sense of obligation.

What was going on there? Jon wondered, and then felt immediately guilty for spying on her. He looked to his hands, noticed the towel, and started drying his hair.

"It's kind of ironic," he said. "I came to Bhutan to learn how to stop feeling other people's emotions. And now this."

Jon knew that Ella was sending a text to Venn, a simple apology about not coming by.

She glanced up. "We need it to be really dry. Wet hair causes lower impedances." She put down her phone and dropped the note in the trash. "I'm sorry, what were you saying?"

Jon repeated himself, the not-so-funny irony of him hoping to disconnect and instead becoming telepathic.

"How were you hoping to learn to block out other people here?" she asked.

"From a Buddhist nun."

Ella wove her fingers through his hair to test its dryness, giving him a gentle massage. He instinctively turned to her, his eyes level with her silver belt buckle.

"When will you meet with her?" she said.

"I met with her last night actually. At Tigers Nest."

"Really?" Ella started fitting the EEG cap on. "What did she say?"

“She talks in riddles. Stuff like, meditate, be clear about what I want, let go. Trust me, I’ve done that plenty of times.”

“Let go of what?”

“My ego, I think, ‘Victory over oneself’ and all that.”

Ella positioned the sensors.

“How do you know a Buddhist nun at Tigers Nest?”

“I came here when I was seven to demonstrate a kind of telepathy with my mom. She also called it tuning in by the way. Neema, that’s the nun’s name, was visiting at the same time.”

“That’s right, I saw it in your profile. Can you and your mom still do that?”

Jon shook his head, the sensors rattling.

“She died of a brain tumor a few months after we got back to Iceland.”

“Oh, I’m so sorry to hear that.”

Ella clipped some cables together and knelt in front of him, as if studying him.

Jon was relieved for the break in the conversation. He could better understand her thoughts when they weren’t talking.

After a moment, he said, “You might be right.”

“What?”

“You were thinking about my connection with my mom.”

“Oh my God, this is just too weird.” Ella closed her eyes, shook her head. “Now I’m going to be paranoid about what I’m thinking.”

"Sorry. But yeah, like you were thinking, maybe I keep myself so open to somehow honor her memory. Or because I think that's why she loved me."

Jon remembered his mother's face lighting up every time he got a number right.

"You said it better than I thought it," Ella said.

"Well, I've thought about this curse of mine a lot. It's given me plenty of alone time."

"Huh, I know about being alone. My daughter Jady lives full-time with her dad. Even a simple chat between us seems to go sideways. You know, sometimes it feels like I have your empath thing too. Not as strong, I'm sure, but I sometimes feel it when something big happens to Jady or someone else I love. Even if we're not together."

"A lot of people say that. Especially married couples and twins."

"It's faint but I notice it. It's also possible that I just notice that stuff more because of my work." Ella sat back on her heels, looking at the wires in her hands. "Anyway, I worry that Jady's got it too. She's so vulnerable, so easily led. And I feel like I'm just letting her down."

Jon took her hand and gave it a gentle squeeze.

Ella stood, wiping away a tear. "Thanks. Hey, I'm supposed to be helping you."

"Okay. Scan away."

She moved behind him to her workstation. "This should be quick. For now, I just want to record your current uh, telepathic state. I cannot believe what I'm saying."

Jon stayed still during the process, imagining what might be going on in his brain.

After less than a minute, Ella gasped. “What the bloody hell. Ninety-three hertz? That can’t be right. Hold on.” She rushed to the bathroom and returned with a hairdryer. She removed the EEG cap and blew dry his hair, the high fan reminding him vaguely of the whistling he’d had before he became fully telepathic. Once the cap was back on, she recorded him again.

“Ninety-four hertz? That’s high gamma.”

Jon felt her rush of excitement and confusion.

“You should be having an epileptic seizure right now.”

Jon couldn’t follow her stream of thought as she processed the scientific implications of her discovery. He did note that that was how she thought of this, *her discovery.* After a few minutes of sitting quietly, he felt physically relaxed and realized that underneath Ella’s emotions and his own fears, he still had the foundation of deep calm.

“It must be a very mild seizure,” he said, deadpan.

“Here, come see the recording.”

With the large cable still connecting his head to her computer, Jon moved slowly. He stood behind her, in her lavender perfume aura, and saw a rapidly oscillating line wave filling the main screen.

“I wonder,” Ella said. She clicked a key to freeze the wave and then zoomed out.

He watched the tight wave pattern shrink, as if it was moving away, until it became a sloping line itself. Ella’s mind raced, estimating the frequency of the new wave.

She continued zooming out and sure enough, the thick line became a long, almost flat, wave pattern itself.

"And there it is," Ella said. "We zoomed out of a super-fast wave to see that it was embedded within an equally slow wave." She pointed to a set of numbers. "One hertz. That's low delta. Like a bass drum, slow and loud." She turned and looked up to him. "Super slow frequencies like delta can be linked with ultra-fast gamma frequencies. These different frequencies can occur together in the same states of meditative consciousness."

Under the best of circumstances, this would have been hard for Jon to follow. Hearing Ella's mind jump to previous research on the esoteric neural oscillations made it nearly impossible. Instead, he thought how this zooming out to see the bigger picture was kind of like when he rose above the confusion of hearing every fleeting thought to reach a level of knowing.

He held up his hand, feeling as if he were back in grade school in Hofn. "So, what does the delta wave state relate to?"

Ella tapped her finger, keeping her eyes to her screen. "It makes total sense. People with a deep sense of empathy show quick bursts of delta waves during empathetic states. But steady delta usually only happens in deep sleep."

She'd ignored his question, her mind churning on how Jon could be functioning at all.

"I've recorded Tibetan monks who can stay conscious in low delta but they're doing a deep meditation called Yoga Nidra or sleep yoga. These are the same guys who do Tumo meditation in the

Himalayas in winter in a thin robe. They can melt the snow around them."

"Well, that must be what I'm doing," Jon said.

"Ha. They're conscious, but they're meditating. Perfectly still. Not kissing people." She smiled up at him, then turned back to the screen. "Hold on a sec."

She toggled between windows, typed in commands and then waited as a progress bar crept from left to right.

"Okay, the program's done. We have a replica of the amplitude and frequency for your right TPJ region while you're telepathic. I might as well make a new binaural beat track."

Ella entered more commands, then stood and paced the room while the program churned. "This is absolutely incredible you know," she said.

Jon heard in her thoughts that she couldn't wait to listen to the new track.

He sat again, wires covering his head, and rubbed his face, wondering when she was going to help him. As if on cue, he heard her notice him and remember their earlier conversation about helping him turn it off.

She came up and knelt in front of him again. "Sorry. I got carried away."

"That's understandable. So, what now? Do we scan again?"

She took his hands and held eye contact with him for a long moment.

Jon heard and felt a change within her, a softening.

"No, this isn't the way."

She gave him the most loving smile he'd seen since he was seven.

"You can let go of your mom now."

After what felt like a few minutes, Ella's thoughts faded away, as if Jon had turned off an insane radio talk show. He held his breath, listening.

Nothing.

He blinked open to see Ella sitting in front of him in her desk chair, her headphones on and her eyes closed.

The computers had gone back to sleep, and the room was peaceful.

He tapped Ella's knee and she took off her headphones, but kept her eyes closed.

"Ella. It worked," he said, almost to himself, as though afraid to jinx it. "I don't hear you anymore."

She sat perfectly still, smiling with her eyebrows raised high. Give her some time to come out, he thought. He admired her beauty and really wanted to kiss her again. He shifted his gaze to the tall windows, to the steady procession of heavy gray clouds lumbering up the valley and speculated if it would rain during his run this evening.

"You can still run in the rain," Ella said.

Jon turned back to find her eyes still shut, her smile wider.

"Yes Jon, I heard you think that."

He sucked in a breath. "What?"

Ella opened her eyes wide and gripped his hands. “This is bizarre!”

“But how—”

“I’ve been listening to the new track I just made. It put me in a deeper state than I’ve ever been, and I felt completely weightless. On a whim, I focused on hearing your thoughts, made it clear that that was what I wanted to do, you know? There was this nasty whistle for a moment like you had described, and then—” she pointed both hands to Jon. “There you were.” She tapped her head. “Here you are.”

Jon didn’t believe her. “That’s amazing. Okay, what am I thinking right now?”

His mind chose to bring up his mother’s small stone Buddha statue which sat on his front porch.

Ella looked away for moment, then told him.

Just as they had done with Ella, they repeated this process a few more times, until his smile became an astonished laugh.

“Ella, what is going on?”

She laughed with him, a crazed look in her eyes.

“I have no idea. You’re right, it’s hard to think like this, and my headache is back with a vengeance.”

Jon couldn’t help but feel invaded, exposed.

“Hey,” Ella said, “Now you know how I felt when you were tuned in to me.”

“Fair enough. Okay, let me try to turn it back on again. We’ll see what it’s like to be tuned in to each other at the same time.” Jon went inward, focused his attention on Ella and after a minute, heard a quick burst of the whistling tone accompanied and then she faded in.

"Something, yeah, yeah there you are," he said. "It worked. I heard the whistle, but it was brief. Imagine hearing that thing non-stop."

"It sounds almost like an old TV turning on." Her voice trailed off as their thoughts took over.

Ella and Jon stared at each other, only slight facial expressions reflecting the most intimate, most confusing experience of their lives: a two-way, instantaneous, direct transference of thought. Their brains struggled to make sense of sharing another stream of consciousness. Like frantic multi-tasking.

For Jon, the initial overwhelming amazement and vulnerability had faded enough for his psychology degree to kick in. He tracked her shifting from one concept to the next and was again fascinated by the racing flow of her mind. Ella's thinking style seemed so similar to his own.

He heard her agree about how similar they were and heard that she was studying his thought patterns as well.

Something resembling a conversation began with split second awareness rather than spoken sentences.

Ella formed sentences in her mind, "We're both focused on listening to each other, but it's not a silent stand-off. So, we're still coming up with enough original thoughts for the other person to hear."

Jon agreed, thinking how the experience was far from silent. Then his mind drifted to considering how this ability could help him as a healer.

"Yes, and it will help my research," Ella thought. "I'll know exactly what people are thinking as I watch their brains light up in an fMRI."

Jon barely heard her; he was too busy imagining an eye gazing session with one of his clients where he heard their every thought.

The telepathic conversation had lasted less than fifteen seconds before they were unable to keep up with each other. Their own thoughts along with the other's person's thoughts were coming too fast.

After a few minutes, Ella said out loud, "This is too much. I need to tune out. How do you turn this off?"

"Thinking about letting my mother go didn't work. But when I stayed calm and thought clearly about wanting to tune out, it happened."

Ella closed her eyes and went inward.

Jon heard her repeating her intention like a mantra, and a moment later she blinked and opened her eyes.

"It worked." She shook her head. "That. Was. Intense."

"Yeah, it's too much. I stayed tuned in to you to hear what happens when you tune out. You just need to set your intention."

Ella jumped to her feet and paced the room. "I have no idea how this is possible or what this means. But I experienced it, so I've got to accept it." She paused at the window, looking out. "We're making history here. Your new recording did it. How did my brain change so fast? It usually takes months for a brain to rewire." She rubbed the side of her head. "I've done brain entrainment for years. Maybe that helped."

Jon felt exhilarated and was pretty sure he was getting the same emotion from Ella. His empath condition remained strong as ever.

Ella gazed out at the vast open vista, her thoughts fluttering like the trapped birds in the lobby. It was hard for Jon to follow, even at the higher knowing level. He gave up trying and thought instead of how at last he knew someone who shared his bizarre experience, the telepathy part at least. She was like a partner to him.

Ella turned, her face set, and crossed the room. "I need some fresh air." She stopped with her hand on the doorknob and turned back. "Did you say something?"

"I don't think so."

"Well, I'm not tuned in to you, but I heard your voice in my head telling me to stay."

They stared in silence.

"Well, I did think that," Jon said. "I wanted you to stay. To keep talking about this." And I thought you might be going to see Venn.

Ella came back from the door. "That's bloody weird. It's like you put a thought in my head." Another pause. "Like my monks sending and receiving messages."

"Let's try it again," Jon said.

"Alright, send me another thought."

Jon tried thinking commands, like for her to raise her arms, to stick out her tongue.

"Nothing," Ella said. "Hmmm, try to recreate the mental state you were in before."

"Well, I really wanted to say something, but didn't."

Ella was standing at her keyboard again. "Here, sit down. I'll start recording so if it happens again, we'll know what's going on in your brain." Then she came in front of him, a peculiar look on her face. Jon picked up from her a mixture of concerns. Were they were moving too fast? Was this dangerous to their health? How did she feel so connected him soon soon?

Jon leaned in and she pulled away. He lifted his hands to bring her close and she held them down. He heard her mind bouncing around, trying to decide what to do.

She leaned in, lightly brushed her lips on his, then stayed an inch from his face, waiting.

Jon put his full attention on one thought: kiss me.

An instant later, her soft lips pressed onto his.

Again, he lost himself in the sensation of what they both felt, but one thought from Ella came through clearly, that she'd heard him.

The front door slammed shut, jolting them back to reality.

Jon turned to see Jeffrey Venn walking toward them.

"Oh, hi," Ella said. "You scared me."

"Don't you move fast," Venn said.

"We were recording." Ella stood and hustled to her keyboard.

Venn watched her bend over her desk and then dragged his gaze away to Jon.

"Nice hat."

Jon held eye contact but kept quiet, trying to keep up with Ella's racing thoughts. He heard from her the same sense of guilt towards Venn, which made him curious. She then shifted her focus, onto something else called epsilon intervals and wanting to measure Jon's heart rate and respiration.

Wearing hiking books and his utility belt with the large knife, Venn came forward in a practiced swagger, keeping his hands in the pockets of his shorts.

So, Jon thought, maybe they *were* going to hike together.

Venn came behind Ella to peer at the screen.

Jon realized he wasn't hearing Venn's thoughts, which meant he didn't automatically hear people around him. He did want to know what Venn was thinking though. He set his intention and quickly tuned out of Ella and then in to Venn, which confirmed that he only heard who he wanted to hear.

The difference in the tone of their thinking was striking, as if he'd switched from Mozart to Guns N' Roses.

"What do you have for me?" Venn said. He stepped closer, brushing against her backside.

Get away from her, Jon thought.

Venn jerked his head to Jon and stared a moment, as if Jon had spoken out loud.

"You two work for me, remember? Ella, what's going on?"

She brought herself up and turned.

Venn didn't move back, and she was trapped between him and her desk, their faces inches apart.

Jon had to say something, had to get Venn away from Ella. "It's incredible, but we have telepathy."

Venn literally laughed in Ella's face, not even looking at Jon. "Oh yeah? That's great. No really, why are you recording him again?"

"He's not kidding."

Venn leaned in to her, almost touching her. "Then what am I thinking right now?"

She leaned back. "It doesn't work like that."

"I've heard that before. You guys really need to get out more."

"I'm ready," Jon said. "Think about an object or a number."

Venn looked to the ceiling.

Jon described a silver sports car.

Venn brought his head down and pulled in his chin. "My Porsche. Good guess."

He turned back to Ella.

To stop them from staring at each other, Jon suggested they do another.

Venn kept staring at her, smiling. "Okay, Gunnarson, what am I thinking about now?"

As though he were reliving his own memory, Jon saw flashes of sex from Venn's perspective. Power and lust coursed through him as he experienced Venn aggressively taking a woman from behind. The woman turned her head, and it was Ella.

"You had sex," Jon said, his voice quiet.

"Yes, we did." Venn still wouldn't look away or move away from Ella. "That's incredible Gunnarson. It really is. I knew you were bullshitting me when you said you couldn't do it. But you're a freak. That's why you're here. Ella, your turn."

Ella closed her eyes a moment and then correctly identified three numbers that Venn thought of.

"Holy shit," he said. "Are you fucking kidding me?"

Jon heard Venn's thoughts shift to revisions of his marketing plan and the media contacts he'd reach out to.

Venn noticed them watching him.

"You still reading my mind?"

"Actually," Jon said, "You only hear the person's thoughts in the moment. You can't get into their memories."

"Well, turn it off." He watched them, looking for some sign of proof.

Venn seemed to Jon even more on edge than he had in their eye gazing session a few days ago, so he stayed tuned in to monitor him. He figured, what was the risk? If he kept his face neutral, how would Venn know?

"I can't believe this," Venn said, laughing as he paced around the room. "My app actually works? This is massive."

"Not exactly," Ella said. "I transformed after listening to a *new* binaural track. A track based on Jon when he was tuned in to me."

"Give me the track. I want to listen to it right now."

"It probably won't work right away. The brain takes a few months to rearrange. I've been doing brain entrainment for years so—"

"I've been into it too. Why do you think I called you in the first place?" He reached past her and picked up her phone. "It's on here?"

Put that down, Jon thought.

Venn dropped the phone. "I just heard you Gunnarson. For the second time." He jabbed his index finger to his temple. "In here."

"We're not sure what that is," Ella said.

"He talked inside my head. That's what it is. What the fuck is going on?"

Jon felt Venn's fury at being trespassed. He hadn't meant to send Venn the message, and he reminded himself to be more careful.

"I told you to turn it off." Venn moved slowly toward him.

Jon's aikido instinct kicked in and he shifted his weight down into the ready position. He heard Venn remember he was a martial arts master.

Venn stopped and grunted. He kept his eyes on Jon now. "Give me the track, Ella."

Ella put her phone in her jeans pocket. "This can't get out there."

"I paid for it. You got your MRI truck. Now I want the track."

"Not this." Ella pointed to the screen, her face tight. "No way. This dramatically changes the human brain, Jeffrey. We need formal testing to know what's happening, what the risks are."

"Enough." Venn shoved his palm toward her. He kept his glare on Jon, unwavering.

It felt to Jon as if Venn's thoughts were boring right into him.

"Gunnarson, if you're still spying in my head then you know I'm not backing down here." He pointed toward Ella and the monitors. "I own that. Tell me Gunnarson, you ready to be sued? Sent home tomorrow?"

Venn's thoughts dominated Jon's mind now, raging like heavy metal rock. A manic, aggressive tension overwhelmed him.

Jon spoke slowly. "We don't have much of a choice here Ella. We have to give him the recordings."

"What?" Ella looked stunned. "Are you kidding? These—"

"Recordings?" Venn's palm shot up again, still glaring at Jon. "There's more than one?"

Jon nodded, his head heavy. Something about the way Venn looked at him compelled him to answer.

"Just before you came in, we recorded my brain while I sent her a message like the one you heard."

Ella covered her eyes with her hand.

"Outstanding," Venn said. "Give me that one too."

He looked over to her and sneered.

"Hey Ella, I bet I can guess what message he sent you. You should watch out for his mind control."

Friday, October 19

Ella woke shortly after midnight to a loud banging on her front door. She rushed to find Venn peering manically back at her through the peephole. Her first thought was that he was in a jealous rage, but when she spotted Oliver and Lex behind him, like sleepy hostages, she reluctantly let them in.

Venn raved that he was hearing her thoughts and proved it to her with a wild gleam in his eyes, like a madman with a powerful new weapon.

"Make tracks for these two," Venn said. "Teach them how to tune in and out."

"Can't we do this in the morning?"

"No, are you kidding? This is massive." He turned to Oliver and Lex. "Like I said, when you hear a high whistle, you'll know it's happening."

"Jeffrey, they should spend weeks, or months, working up to the hyper gamma waves in Jon's new track."

Venn came close, his breath stale. "We don't have weeks or months."

Ella obeyed but couldn't figure out why he seemed so desperate. If his app really did made people telepathic, he should be ecstatic, not unhinged like this.

After thirty minutes of listening, Oliver and Lex had such severe headaches, they gave up, gulped down the rest of her ibuprofen, and left. Venn remained, pacing as he always did, looking at her in a way that made her conscious of her thin t-shirt and PJ shorts.

She moved to the front door. "Okay, well, I'm really tired and have an early flight."

"What? You can't leave now."

"Yeah, my flight's in about six hours."

"Ella, come on. We're changing the world here, and you're leaving?"

"I promised my daughter I'd be home—"

"What? Are you kidding me?"

Ella opened the door and chilly air ran across her bare feet and legs.

"Well, bring her here, if you have to. I'll pay for it."

She shook her head, thinking it made no sense to bring Jady all the way here with school resuming on Monday.

"Plus, a twenty-five-thousand-dollar bonus for you. Just through Monday."

She gave a tight smile, to show she appreciated his offer, but shook her head again.

"All the videos and the web site. We have to redo it all."

"Okay, but I can't do it today, Jeffrey. What's the rush? And remember, this recording can't be put on the market until it's been tested for health risks."

Venn shut his eyes and took a deep breath.

"Of course." He spoke slowly and softly now. "It's just that, while you're here, with Jon, on location, we should do what we can. And you're the star, Ella." He came close and held her shoulders. "You'll be the most famous scientist in the world. Think what this will do for your career."

He did make a good point, she conceded. George was returning to London today, which meant Jady could stay with him over the weekend. Once they heard what was happening here, they'd certainly understand her change in plans. "Okay, okay, but you need to go now. I have a wicked headache and I have to get some sleep. We'll talk in the morning."

Ella emerged from a deep sleep at eight, with the half-awake, fleeting hope—and fear—that yesterday had been a bizarre dream. Then she remembered kissing Jon, which she knew had to be real. But everything after that moment still felt like a movie. It was all as strange as if she'd started levitating or walking on the ceiling.

She headed to the bathroom and splashed ice-cold mountain water on her face.

Time to tell Wendell, her department head, she thought. How, exactly was she going to do it? This wasn't the type of finding you could just fire off in an email. And what could she say? What did she know, really?

Based on the night before, it seemed that only people who'd done regular brain entrainment would become telepathic immediately. She still had no earthly idea how Jon had transformed. He'd said that quick flashes of telepathy had been happening for the past few days, and that he'd become fully telepathic the instant they'd first kissed. She knew it was outrageous, but she considered that something about their close proximity and powerful emotions must have done something to his brain, like maybe the mirror neurons in the TPJ region. She had to get him in an fMRI.

But how, scientifically, could telepathy be possible at all, she wondered. "Nothing violates the core theory of physics," Wendell would say. "No magic allowed." He'd be right, nothing immaterial could influence something material like a brain.

She squeezed toothpaste and brushed side to side, being gentle on her gums and grateful for a familiar activity.

There had to be an extremely weak, long-range force or field that science hadn't yet detected, she reasoned. Much weaker than gravity. Waves in this kind of field would have almost no ability to move objects, but they could still carry a lot of information.

She rinsed out her mouth.

Still, the brain as a sense organ?

Ella decided to hold off on sharing her news with her colleagues until she had at least a vague sense of what was happening. It was only three in the morning in London, so she had some time to figure a piece of it out.

Thinking of London brought up Jady and George, and an all too familiar guilt. She leaned on the sink, heavy on her hands, and tried to assure herself they'd understand. Her puffy, red eyes in the mirror made her feel even more exhausted and her headache worse. She again wished she still had the MRI truck to see what the hell was going on in her own brain.

She brewed strong coffee and sat on her bed to review the promotional schedule and new scripts. Basically, she and Jon would be demonstrating telepathy like trick monkeys. He also had to do an instructional video called "Click Up from the Chatter: Rise to the Level of Knowing." Good luck with that one, Jon, she thought.

Her front door slammed and a moment later she heard Jeffrey barking orders to Gautam, the videographer from the day before. She deeply regretted giving him a card key to her cabin. Staring at her bedroom door, half-expecting it to swing open at any moment, she considered how different Jeffrey and Jon were, from each other and from other men in general. As if the space around them was charged with their unique signals.

Until yesterday, being with Jeffrey had felt like visiting a hot nightclub—kind of cheesy, but also sexy and exciting. Now he just felt crazy, maybe dangerous. Being with Jon felt a bit like a day at the spa—a chance to truly let go. But still, he should have backed her up about not giving Jeffrey the recordings.

Half an hour later, she emerged from her bedroom, again feeling silly in her teal surgery shirt and white doctor jacket. Thankfully, Jeffrey had left, but Gautam was stretching to raise a light and Oliver sat at his desk picking at his face. She didn't like living in a public space but told herself that she'd better get used to having no privacy.

Oliver saw her approach and darted his hand to the mouse. He jerked back as she arrived, as if he'd closed a program just in time. "This is crazy, right?" He leaned back, searching her face.

She made a point of not looking at his screen.

"More videos, huh?" he said.

"Yes, more bloody videos."

"And Jeffrey wants them live before London wakes up," he said.

"As though one extra day makes any difference," Ella said. Saying it out loud, it dawned on her that Venn had no intention of testing the recording.

Oliver chuckled. "What if I tuned in to my mum and dad when they were waking up? Hearing them thinking about taking a pee and making tea."

Ella's belly tightened. "We'd tell people when we tuned in. Don't you think? Otherwise, it would be like eavesdropping."

"Huh. Yeah, I suppose." He played with a pimple on his cheek. "Oh, Jeffrey says that the second new recording you gave him isn't working. He wants you and Jon to teach him how to send thoughts."

"Send thoughts?"

"That's what he calls it when Jon talks in someone else's head." The pimple was now bleeding onto his fingernail.

Ella nodded, grateful Oliver couldn't hear her thoughts.

By midday, and with the first two videos complete, Ella finally had the room to herself. This helped her believe that she also had her mind to herself, until she remembered they'd established the night before that telepathy didn't degrade with distance. Jon or Jeffrey could be spying on her at any time.

What was she to do? Stop thinking altogether? Only think benign things? What if she had secrets to keep?

Regarding secrets, she realized she could tune in to Jeffrey. She did and immediately heard him discussing the Tuning In launch with Lex. She knew she had to do something to stop him.

After getting nowhere with the local police, she contacted the Consular Warden, the British Ambassador to Bhutan. The best she got from his office was that he might be able to meet with her in the late afternoon.

She hung up the phone and drifted to her usual thinking spot at the window. Towers of clouds stood motionless in the valley, as if waiting for something.

Leaning her forehead on the cool glass, she considered how telepathy was going to change the world. Jeffrey was right, she'd be famous. However, knowing her peers, if Jon's recordings were released into the market without testing, she'd be criticized as being irresponsible. Her career would be over, a career she'd sacrificed everything for.

She looked to the pine needles below and imagined her forehead piercing through the pane, her body falling in a shower of glass.

Jady would become telepathic too. How would she possibly survive that? A girl devastated when she didn't get enough likes on a social media post would soon hear Becca think her ass looked big. She'd hear Peter checking out another girl. And what about sending thoughts? Ella could not let that second recording out.

She pushed her forehead, hard, into the glass.

Her phone vibrated in her pocket with an incoming text. It was from her friend Victoria, Becca's mum.

"Call me right away," it read.

Ella did the quick math and wondered why Vic would be texting her at seven a.m., London time. She called her, using the hotel phone on her desk.

Victoria answered on the first ring, her voice controlled but curt. "Hello, Ella? Our daughters were picked up by the police in Wellington Square last night. Both of them stinking drunk."

"What? How?"

"They snuck out. Becca has never done anything like this before," she said, as if Jady were the bad influence. "We need you to pick up Jady. Right away."

"I can't. But George should be home soon."

"No, I've already spoken to him. He's out of the country until the middle of next week."

Vic had called George first, Ella realized, even though they were close friends, and even though she was the mom. "No, his trip ended yesterday."

"He turned his business trip into a long weekend, something about seeing the fall colors in New England. His new girlfriend's joining him. He said you'd be on your way home."

George must have emailed her (he preferred email to texts) and with everything going on, Ella hadn't checked.

"What time to do you land?" Victoria said.

"I'm still in Bhutan. I'm here through Monday. Something incredible's happened, Vic. We've discovered telepathy."

Vic made a huffing sound. "Ella, your beautiful, fifteen-year-old daughter was passed out drunk in the middle of Chelsea at one in the morning. She looks dreadful. Whatever nonsense you're up to with your monks can wait."

This couldn't be happening right now, Ella thought, her mind racing. She remembered Venn's offer to bring Jady here and, in a flash, decided that this would be the perfect place for her and Jady to hide out and reconnect as Tuning In took off.

"Vic, I need your help, I'm bringing Jady here."

###

Jon needed a fight. That morning in the Beyul restaurant, on his way to the restroom, a sprinting toddler and a busy busboy had converged on him. He'd instantly pivoted and shifted in the only possible way to avoid a collision. That quick move had brought back years of training and, for the first time since he lost to Neema, he *needed* to practice aikido.

He sat in the back seat of the stuffy Nalu Resort van waiting for Jigme, the driver, to come back out of the resort and take him to Thimphu, the capital of Bhutan.

Jigme appeared, and to Jon's surprise, Ella followed close behind. She looked deeply troubled, and as she approached the vehicle and spotted him, she paused for a second as though unsure if she wanted to be in the same van as him.

"No tuning in," she said by way of a greeting, as she slid into the row behind him.

Jigme wound them down the hillside, filling the silence with a cautionary weather report. They rolled to a stop just inside the resort gate for two cows who'd selected this shady spot for a rest. Jigme hopped out armed with a riding crop and let the cows know he was there, with a gentle tap.

Jon realized that his chest and shoulders were tight, and his entire body felt heavy. Ella was indeed deeply troubled, about multiple, seemingly unrelated issues.

He decided to start slow. "Where are you headed?"

"Thimphu."

"I thought you were leaving today."

"Nope."

Jigme whistled and swatted the cows to coax them onto their feet.

It occurred to Jon that he should have known she wasn't leaving. He and Ella had worked together for three hours that morning without exchanging more than polite conversation. Sure, he'd told Venn about the recordings the night before, but she'd slept with the asshole.

"Are you kidding?" she said, leaning forward, grabbing the back of his seat. "Giving him those recordings is so much worse."

"I thought you said, no tuning in?"

Jigme was pushing on one of the cow's backside.

"I suppose I didn't want you tuning in to me. I can't handle it right now."

Jon thought how unfair, how rude this was and was glad she could hear him.

"Alright, alright," she said. "I'm tuning out."

Jon watched Jigme talking to the cows, the beasts lumbering to their feet.

"Okay, I'm out," she said. "But really, Jon, why did you side with Jeffrey about giving him the tracks yesterday?"

"I don't know." He turned around to face her. "I was tuned in to him and it was like I got swept up by his thoughts. He has this—" Jon searched for the right word. "Presence. It makes him hard to refuse."

"Yes, I can relate to that."

Jigme hopped back in, smiling as usual. "Waa haa," he said. "Now we have that out of the way, we have a nice drive together."

And they were off.

Jon moved back to Ella's row, and she scooted to make room.

"He's moving too fast," she said. "His team's already pushed out your updated recording for the app. I think it's because he's worried about getting shut down."

Jon gave her a puzzled look.

"After breakfast," Ella said, "Lex and he were having one of their arguments on the deck at Beyul, so I tuned in to him. Turns out the FBI's after him for Internet fraud. It seemed like he's been doing it for years. It sounded like his court hearing is next Tuesday and he's flying back to New York on Monday."

"Whoa." Jon's first eye-gazing session with Venn now made perfect sense.

"He told Lex that Person8 would probably be shut down and she flipped over a table. Plates and glasses and all. Jeffrey did the same thing to another table, like he couldn't be outdone."

"They're quite the pair," Jon said.

"You think?"

They shared a laugh.

"And how about their outfits," Ella said. "The whole Tomb Raider thing?"

"The what?"

"You know, the video game and the movies. Very violent. Jady loved it."

"Is that why he sometimes calls her Lara?"

"Yes, exactly. Bizarre, right? It was funny at first, but it's like she really thinks she is Lara Croft. Like this is some kind of action movie."

"I'm avoiding her altogether," Jon said.

"She tasered me. I really can't wait for them to get the hell out of here."

"So, if Person8's shut down, that would put an end to the app, right?"

"Yes, I suppose, but it may not be in time. He's spending buckets of money on adverts right now, especially to people who already have other entrainment or meditation apps. It's crazy, but in a few weeks, millions of people could have an app that will actually make them telepathic."

Jigme pointed to the towering clouds, speculating whether it would rain that afternoon in Thimphu.

Jon politely acknowledged him, and then came back to their conversation. "Remember that nun I told you about? Neema?"

Ella nodded.

"She said we can change, transform ourselves by going inward. What if she meant *we* as in everyone, like, all of humanity transforming?"

Ella frowned, watching the road in front of them.

"My transformation happened without any entrainment," Jon said. "I'm sure there are others out there like me. Like that autistic kid in LA. And, supposedly, millions of people hear voices."

"What are you saying?"

"Think about it, everyone has serendipity with friends or family, you know, like, oh-my-God-I-was-just-thinking-about-you? And these completely random thoughts that pop into our heads. Where do they come from? This might have been happening slowly for a long time."

Ella squinted, her brows drawn together. "What's been happening?"

"Humans evolving toward telepathy. It might not be a such bad thing. It might be natural development."

"Evolution should take generations, Jon. Not a mobile app. And even if telepathy was part of our evolutionary path, this accelerates it too much."

"This is the main road," Jigme said. "We go faster now."

"Jon, species can't handle sudden, dramatic changes like this. Mass telepathy could be for us what the asteroid was for the dinosaurs."

Jon considered her point. He'd been cursed with something almost like telepathy his whole life and yesterday it had still overwhelmed him. But what if humanity survived it? How would the world be different?

"And you know Venn's not going to stop," Ella said, louder now. "He's going to make a fortune."

Jigme glanced in the rearview mirror with obvious concern. He announced in a near yell that he'd drop Jon off first. "Babesa Middle School. Right, Mr. Gunnarson?"

"Yes, thank you."

"You're going to a school?" Ella said, blinking.

"Yeah, meeting some karate fighters in the gym. It's been almost three weeks since I've practiced aikido and I miss it. I tracked down a couple of guys who teach afterschool karate programs. They represented Bhutan in the Summer Olympics in Tokyo."

"Hmm, doesn't sound very fair to me."

"I'll be okay."

"No, I mean, fair to them. You're going to be hearing their thoughts, right? They don't stand a chance."

"I won't tune in to them without telling them. And anyway, aikido's all about bringing you and your attacker to safety, not about hurting the other guy."

Ella only nodded.

The van slowed and was quiet for a mile, except for Jigme spitting betel nut shells into a plastic cup.

"By the way, I don't know how you can do it," Ella said, "Your baseline brain state is gamma waves, which are very inefficient. I'd expect you to be exhausted."

"You know, I was pretty tired the past couple days. And starving. But I feel good today."

"We'll have to measure you again. Maybe your brainwaves have lowered. Or maybe you're accommodating to a new normal."

Jon shrugged. "How are you holding up? You didn't seem too happy about the videos this morning."

"Uh, no. My colleagues will think I'm a reckless hack. My boss is on holiday in France and won't return my calls or emails."

Jon realized he hadn't told anyone. Then he wondered who'd he even tell.

"So, I'm trying to stop Jeffrey," she said. "I'm heading to Thimphu to hopefully meet with the British Ambassador. He's not back in his office until late afternoon. I was going to walk around town while I waited. I had to get out of that resort."

"You're welcome to come see some aikido."

"Watch you wrestle around? And miss the shopping in Thimphu?" Ella smiled and took his hand. "I'd like that."

Jigme hummed a tuneless melody, not even trying to pass a horse-drawn cart they were following.

"I haven't called my parents yet," Ella said, "But I did reach an old friend and gave her a demonstration. Scared the life out of her."

"It's going to take some time."

"Meanwhile, Jeffrey's selling fifty thousand units a day. For all we know, it could be giving people brain tumors. We have to do something, Jon."

He felt her anxiety building and thought how this could be his first telepathic healing session. "Let's tune in."

Ella gave his hand a quick squeeze to signal her okay.

He closed his eyes and after the usual brief whistling, Ella's thoughts faded in.

They opened their eyes and stared at each other, swaying with the slow motion of the van. Jon kept his own thoughts as quiet as he could and, after a few minutes, her thought pattern became clear. She was caught in a loop of fear and guilt about Venn's reckless exploitation of their discovery. As an occasional undercurrent, she also had a deep concern for her daughter, Jady.

Jon allowed her feelings to flow in and through him, as though observing from a distance. He wasn't sure if it was because his brain had changed or if he was following Neema's advice of not resisting but, either way, it wasn't so bad.

He pointed out her thinking pattern as it happened and helped her break free. Together, their sense of time dissolved and their minds floated as if in a hot air balloon, rising far above the world.

Jigme called Jon's name to say they'd arrived.

The ninety-minute drive had passed in a moment, as though they'd had a deep sleep. Jon heard Ella think that she didn't want to stop. "I know," Jon said, "But we should tune out now."

Babesa Middle School spread across a gentle hill a few miles south of the capital city Thimphu. They wound between spotless buildings and dusty fields to a new looking gymnasium with a teal metal roof.

Jon climbed out of the van and stretched. He recognized the loud slap of mat tiles being stacked inside and took the stairs three at a time. Even before his eyes had adjusted to the room, he spotted the two bright white robes. The smell of wood floor polish filled the cool, dusty air, taking him back to his high school gym in Iceland. Wearing a broad smile, he strode over to the two men.

The karate fighters paused, each holding a weathered interlocking foam tile. Both of the men had smooth round faces and close-cropped hair. The larger man glanced to the stack of blue tiles in front of him as if gauging whether they'd taken apart too much of their mat to bother rebuilding. He turned his gaze to the door, stood straighter, and then sighed, as though seeing Ella had convinced him it was worth putting the mat back together.

Jon apologized for being late. His explanation that there'd been construction seemed a statement of the obvious.

Puran, likely in his early forties and easily the largest Bhutanese man Jon had ever seen, made it clear that he soon needed to be somewhere else. It was Friday afternoon after all.

Dorji looked a bit younger and he smiled non-stop, especially at Ella.

The men knelt and carefully fit together the teeth of the tiles to rebuild the mat.

Jon walked with Ella to a wobbly red plastic chair positioned next to a humming water fountain and directly under a framed picture of the king and queen. He slipped out of his sandals, handed Ella his phone and money clip and stretched his arms over his head.

Ella and the royal couple watched him with polite smiles.

"So?" And she meant, *are you going to tell them?*

Jon shook his head. "Don't have time to get into that. This'll be quick and then we'll go for a walk around town."

Fifteen minutes later, Jon came back to the water fountain, more to give Puran and Dorji a break than because he needed a drink.

Ella seemed amused, as if she'd watched three grown men dance together rather than a martial arts fight. She waved him close, kept her voice low.

"Why are they letting you toss them around like that?"

"It's called aikido, Ella."

"I know, but they're both coming at the same time. How's that possible?"

"One more," Puran called from the mat.

Jon held up a finger to him, asking for a minute to collect his thoughts. These fighters, while highly skilled, clearly weren't one with him and the space around them. But soon they'd likely be telepathic, everyone would be. Jon had to know what that meant in a fight. He knew he wouldn't hurt them, but he also knew it was a risk for him. A familiar thrill ran through his torso and down to his fingertips and Jon considered, as he had while taking the shortcut along the ridge to Tiger's Nest, whether something was wrong with him for taking risks like this.

Yes, he'd promised Ella that he'd let them know if he tuned in, but he only had a few more minutes here. He tuned in to Puran and was surprised at the strength of the man's rage and humiliation. It seemed he'd never fought an aikido master and wasn't used to being so easily controlled.

Jon stood in a relaxed, ready pose as his opponents circled him slowly. The first strikes came together, with loud, growling shouts that echoed in the gym. Jon immediately understood this was no longer a casual practice session. The frustrated karate fighters came with everything they had, full speed, full strength.

Jon marveled at Puran's thoughts; the raw, indecipherable instinct and the occasional burst of Bhutanese inner dialog. And as he did, Dorji's shin slammed into Jon's kidney from behind, bending him forward.

Puran screamed as he whipped his leg up, striking Jon's nose with the top of his foot.

Jon's head exploded with a loud cracking sound. He lost control of his body and crumpled to the mat, the pain instant and sharp. Even under the agony, he still felt Puran's primal thrill, a dizzy adrenaline buzz.

He rose to his hands and knees. Thick red drops were splattering onto the mat under his face.

Puran yelled for Dorji to bring a towel, his thrill ebbing away.

With a detached sense of clarity, Jon realized that just as his own thoughts had distracted him in his fight with Neema, Puran's thoughts had distracted him here, pulled him out of the zone.

Ella's sneakers appeared, and her hand came on his back.

Another stupid risk, he thought. Like nearly slipping over a cliff for the sake of a short cut.

Puran helped him up, his primal thrill now completely gone. Dorji presented Jon a towel of questionable cleanliness to press on his bloody and shattered nose.

No more stupid risks, Jon thought. No more.

Saturday, October 20

Jon didn't think it made any sense. Propped up in bed, an ice pack to his nose, he mulled over his second aikido loss in as many fights. Why had tuning in to Puran made it so difficult? After all, aikido was about becoming one with your attacker. And what better way to do that than by hearing their thoughts? It didn't make sense.

Of course, nothing made sense. Even for someone as accustomed to strangeness as Jon, everything felt too strange and was happening too fast.

He lumbered to the bathroom and eased off the bandage to examine his nose in the mirror. Thankfully, it was a simple fracture; the swelling had almost gone, and he could breathe through it again. And it had gotten him out of the scheduled media interviews. Venn's campaigns portrayed Jon as a more highly evolved human, an enlightened prophet, and a freshly broken nose didn't support that image. Naturally, Venn had yelled at him, asking what the fuck he'd been thinking.

Jon still didn't have a very good answer for that. His phone dinged with a text from Venn asking for an update. Jon realized that Ella hadn't replied to his texts. He considered what he'd done to make her avoid him. He replayed their afternoon together the day before and came up with at least two good reasons. He had to find her and apologize.

He started to tune in to her to figure out where she was but it felt like a invasion of her privacy. Instead he tried putting himself in her shoes. She probably still wanted to be alone, so she wouldn't be in her cabin, the Beyul restaurant, or the Nalu bar. She'd also wanted to reach out to her colleagues, so the spa or a hike were unlikely.

Which left the meditation huts at the top of the waterfall.

It was easy to know which hut Ella was in—the one with a "Shhh" sign on the handle. Jon knocked, announced himself, and she invited him in. She sat cross-legged, holding her phone in the middle of the floor, as if she'd intended to meditate but her device had gotten the best of her.

"How'd you know I was in here?"

Jon shrugged. "Just figured it out."

Her look made him feel guilty, even though he knew he wasn't.

"How's your nose?" She finally said.

"Getting better, thanks." Jon came fully into the hut and let the bamboo door swing shut behind him.

"Kinda makes you look tough."

Jon started to laugh and then grimaced.

Ella smiled, her eyes caring.

Jon thought how she didn't smile nearly enough. He knelt in front of her. "Hey, Ella, I was a total fool yesterday. I'm sorry for tuning in to those guys after I promised I wouldn't. And I'm sorry you missed your chance to meet with the Ambassador."

Ella leaned forward, onto her knees, and gave him a hug.

The two waterfalls pounded outside in steady, mesmerizing stereo sound.

Her body felt strong and soft at the same time.

"I understand," she said, ending the hug and sitting back down. "It's all very bizarre, isn't it, what's happening?"

Jon nodded, still feeling the afterglow of their embrace.

"Here, see this," she said, handing him her phone. "You won't believe it. I'm copied on the Tuning In status emails. He put a one-year money back guarantee on it and sales are taking off. The app's already going viral."

Jon scrolled through a series of graphs, each spiking up and to the right.

Ella reached over and scrolled down the email. "Here are some Tweets and Facebook posts. People complaining of headaches and some saying their telepathy's making them crazy. This isn't only Jeffrey's fault, Jon. We're also responsible for making it happen."

"Wow," he said. "Yeah, you're right."

"My head's spinning right now. I need to do some stretching in here, so I can think straight, okay?"

Ella took child's pose on the firm cushion that covered the entire eight-foot square floor.

"Okay. Good spot for it." He watched her back rise and fall with her breath. "I'll be outside. Thinking thoughts."

Jon sat on a boulder near the top of the booming waterfall. He imagined Ella stretching in the hut and resisted the urge to go back in and try to kiss her again. He told himself that he should be focused on how to stop Venn. The obvious way to start was to tune in to him.

He closed his eyes and almost immediately Venn's mind faded in. It sounded especially noisy, even for him. But above the din, Jon heard him repeating the phrase, *let Jeffrey Venn go,* like a mantra.

Stunned, Jon at first thought Venn was trying to let go of his ego but then realized it didn't feel anything like that. He heard a second stream of thoughts, faint, but definitely there and he realized it must be the mind of someone else Venn was tuned in to.

A moment later, Venn stopped the strange mantra, and the second stream of thoughts faded away. Venn seemed to be researching something, and Jon heard a name that sounded like Jean Olsen or Wolfson, something about Agent in Charge and New York Field Office. He heard Venn restart the audio track and briefly focus on the humming binaural beat.

As before, another faint stream of thoughts arose, and Venn began repeating the same phrase from before. Jon went deeper, to the level of knowing, and knew that Venn was trying to get out of trouble with the FBI. Venn was sending thoughts to FBI agents to try and sway them to let him go.

Jon didn't stop to consider whether it would work, he jumped straight to concern. He'd told Venn about sending thoughts and now he was using that technique to avoid arrest.

The mantra, *let Jeffrey Venn go,* continued. Jon remembered how hard it had been for him to purposefully send Ella a thought and was amazed Venn could send thoughts so well, even if he was listening to the recording while he did it. He wondered how Venn got that last recording.

Ella had said she gave him a fake version, but now Jon questioned whether that was true. He had to ask her.

"Hey Jon," Ella called from the hut, "Can you come here?"

Climbing off the rock, he couldn't help but notice the timing of her calling him and he thought to himself, and possibly to her, that it wasn't okay to tune in without asking. They'd have to promise to only tune in to each other with the other person's approval, otherwise, how could any relationship survive telepathy? As he slid open the hut door, he was determined to talk about it. And to ask her whether she'd given Venn the last recording of him sending thoughts.

Ella was crouching in a frog pose. She faced away from him, her elbows on the padded floor, her knees wide, and her pink running shorts held high. She looked back to her feet. "Do my legs look right? This feels too easy."

The sight before him wiped Jon's mind clean. A complete reset. He took her question at face value and saw that while her knees were spread wide, her body was, in fact, too far forward. He knelt behind her and pulled her hips back a few inches, her shorts soft and warm on his fingers.

"You need to make right angles with your legs," he said.

Ella gave a low moan. "I'm so tight from all the sitting."

Jon gently massaged her hips with his thumbs.

"Mmm, that feels good."

A part of Jon's mind, wired from years ago in his father's smelly pick-up at the Hofn graveyard, tried warning him not to get involved any deeper.

Still, his hands moved.

His practical side warned him that he didn't have time for this right now. He should be asking her how Venn had gotten the last recording.

His thumbs snuck down her glutes. Which were nicely firm.

She tilted her hips up and lowered slightly. "Oh, a massage," she said, "That's a better idea." The left side of her face rested on the floor and her lips puckered. "Ooh, easy there. Hey, tune in to me so you know how it feels."

Jon tuned in and felt from her the deep stretching sensation from the pose. As he rubbed, he felt the tender spots, almost as if he were giving himself a massage. His palms came fully on her rear, his thumbs near the inside of her thighs. At that point, another part of his body took charge. He turned her over and kissed her, this time a mouth-devouring kind of kiss.

Ella was tuned in to him as well and their lovemaking was a truly unified experience. They felt the desires and sensations in each other's bodies almost equally to their own.

Not long after he was inside her, Jon noticed her sensations shift, starting with a weakness in her limbs then a tightness building in her lower belly. Slow, warm waves rolled up inside her from the top of her thighs. The waves quickened and, for them both, a familiar feeling eased in. Like being close to a satisfying yawn or a powerful sneeze.

He moved in a steady rhythm above her, his breath coming faster, and the strong urgency in his own body rose to command his attention. Something deep down told him hold himself back.

"Let go," she whispered in his ear.

They both held their breath and felt every muscle tighten in their bodies.

Ella gasped quick, moaning breaths.

Jon felt multiple waves within her, running up from deep inside her belly, warm and all consuming.

He pulled out at the last possible second as an immense wave of relief washed through him.

Ella's waves of bliss became calmer, and then subsided, flooding relaxation through both of them like a sigh. Her thighs trembled, and they melted into the padded floor as one.

After a time, when they'd stopped panting, Jon heard that his weight on her was becoming too much. He rolled onto his back, satiated, and couldn't help thinking, "Savasana."

Ella laughed and turned to him, resting her head on his shoulder.

"Tuned in sex is pretty frickin amazing," he said.

"Mmmm."

"And you women are lucky. Damn."

"Well, now you can have it too."

They were quiet for a moment, lying side by side. He studied the thatched ceiling and felt her heart beating against him. Her thoughts sped from how wonderful their lovemaking had been and how happy she was to have met him to worrying about her daughter. He felt awkward hearing her most private thoughts and so tuned out.

Back to only his own thoughts, he noticed that his nose was hurting. He tapped it and found blood on his fingers. The cut had reopened in their fit of passion. "Tuned in fighting's not so amazing though."

"Serves you right for not telling them."

"I guess you're right."

"The difference was night and day," she said, "I don't think you should try that again, or you might get yourself killed."

"Yeah. My sensei always said how our thoughts distract. Which must be doubly true of someone else's thoughts."

He'd just tuned out of Ella and already he wished he knew what she was thinking.

"I was thinking," she said, right on cue, "About whether you sent thoughts to your opponents' yesterday."

"I don't know. I doubt it. Speaking of that, Venn's figured out how to send thoughts, and he's using it to try to get out of being arrested."

"What?" Ella sat up. She reached for her t-shirt.

A part of Jon wished he'd stayed quiet a moment longer. But then he realized she would have heard him think about Venn anyway.

"We shouldn't be lying around," she said. "We've got to do something. We need him to get arrested, so the app will be stopped."

Jon fumbled with his underwear. "It sounded like he needs to listen to my last recording to able to send thoughts."

Ella pulled her shorts on and stood over him. "Then to stop him, we have to get that recording back. We'll need to get his phone and his laptop, and any thumb drives we can find."

"What if he backed it up in the cloud?" Jon said.

She sighed and shook her head.

Jon stood, and they faced each other, close in the dark, musty hut. He had to ask. "How did this happen?"

Ella's eyes wandered with a faraway look.

Jon continued, "How did Venn get the recording of me sending you a thought?"

"I have no idea. I gave him a fake. Come on, it's stuffy in here, let's go out."

Again, he wished he'd been tuned in to her. He wondered if this was how it was going to be from now on, making sure to tune in to someone before you asked big questions.

###

Ella stepped out into the blinding sun. Jon was right behind her, pulling on his t-shirt. "We've got to tell the FBI what's going on. Let's go to your cabin to make some calls."

She tilted her head back to put on a ponytail and saw movement at the railing above. Lex was peering down on them from the steps up to the Nalu Bar. She was sick of Lex spying on her. Emboldened by Jon's presence, she was about to yell something like, "leave me alone," but Lex jerked her head back before she could.

She hurried with Jon away from the huts, her mind switching back to how they should alert the FBI. They rounded the corner from the patio and came onto to the path.

Suddenly, Lex was upon them. For the next ten seconds, every movement, every expression seemed to play out in slow motion. Yet also far too fast to fully comprehend and respond to.

Lex was pushing her taser into Jon's left side, the gun making a fast clicking sound. Jon was backing away, feebly trying to grab her arm and moaning, his mouth open wide. And then her beautiful, strong Jon was tumbling backward over the low railing and disappearing down into the small ravine.

She heard a heavy thump and then a rustling sound from the rocks and bushes below. Ella started to the railing, to scale down and help him, but Lex had turned to face her, holding up the huge knife in her other hand.

"This one's for you, bitch."

Seeing no way to get past Lex and reach the narrow path, Ella lurched backward onto the patio.

Lex casually holstered her taser and stepped forward slowly, as if to reinforce the fact that she had Ella trapped.

"No. No," Ella said. "What are you doing, Lex?" She scanned for possible escape: the sheer walls of the gorge, the thatched huts with their flimsy latch doors, and the smaller slippery waterfall in the back. She bumped up against the railing at the edge of the main waterfall. Glancing over, she knew that falling to the sharp rocks thirty feet below would mean instant death.

She scrambled onto the first of the ten boulders that lined the lip of the falls, thinking that if she could get across, the drop on the far side might not be as abrupt. She didn't dare risk hopping across the wet rocks but moved as quickly as she could on her hands and knees, terrified that at any moment she'd feel a slashing cut to her back or legs.

Halfway across, a gust of wind nudged her and blew cold spray on her face and arms. Seeing the water surging over the side, so close beneath her, gave her a dizzy wobbliness. She gripped the stone, not able to move for a moment.

Lex grabbed her ankle.

Ella kicked in panic and was able to free her leg and leap like a frog the five remaining boulders to reach the stone wall on the far side. The cliff there fell nearly straight down and the slick wall above her offered no chance of scaling. She was trapped.

Lex leapt from the middle boulder to the next, as confidently as if jumping between paving stones on a path. She landed strong and stopped to stare at Ella with maniacal intensity. "You're going over!"

Ella imagined trying to wrestle with the powerful Lex on the slippery rocks and knew it was hopeless. She was going to die here. "Lex, please stop. Whatever I've done, I'm sorry."

"Whatever you've done? You fucking whore!" Lex was screaming now, her voice echoing in the gorge.

All at once Jon's head and hands appeared, as he pulled himself up and over the railing and onto the path.

Lex turned back to see what Ella was looking at. Her shoulders dropped and the knife came down to her side.

Jon shuffled onto the patio, unsteady on his feet. His face and shirt were covered in blood. But he still wore a determined look that matched Lex's in intensity.

Lex spun back to Ella, the hatred still there, and turned up one side of her mouth, as if realizing that Jon wouldn't be able to get to them before she did what she needed to do. She started to move again but suddenly, inexplicably, jerked her head back to Jon, as though he'd yelled at the top of his lungs.

Lex kept looking back to him for an odd, still moment. Then, her body rigid, her gaze locked on his, she let herself fall slowly backward and down. Even over the rushing water, Ella heard a sickening crack as she landed.

Jon turned to Ella, his eyes wide. Then he leaned over the railing and peered down.

Ella wasn't sure she could look right now. She felt frozen in place. Crawling back across the boulders was inconceivable after what she'd just witnessed.

"Ella," Jon called, snapping her out of it. "Swim here. Come on, it's okay."

The ice-cold water literally took her breath away and forced her to move. As she reached the middle, the strong current pushed her toward the boulders. She used her hands and feet on the rocks to reach the other side. Shivering and panting, she leaned into his arms.

"Oh, my God, Jon. She was really going to kill me. I thought I was going to die. Oh my God, oh my God."

"It's okay now. She's gone, she's dead."

She squeezed into him, as if to become one, the sun warm on her back. After a moment, she felt the blood on his shirt, sticky on her cheek, and she pulled away.

"Are you alright? Let me see your head."

"I think so. I think it's just a bad cut."

"Let's get you to a hospital."

"And we need to call the police."

Jon turned to leave, but Ella held back.

"Wait. I have to see for myself."

She went to the railing, leaned over as Jon had and stared for a long moment, trying to make sense of all that had happened. Lex's back bent impossibly over the rocks; her bare belly pointed to the sky. The water below her was turning pink. Ella turned away.

"What did you do?" she said. "How did you make her do that?"

"I didn't. I mean, I have no idea what happened."

"You don't think you… made her?"

"What? No."

Jon seemed insulted, so she didn't press it. Still, Ella continued to wonder if he had killed Lex, and what powers he truly possessed. She found herself equally scared and energized by the question. "Well, whatever happened, thank you."

He glanced back over the edge again, as if to change the subject, and tensed.

Ella looked too, terrified that Lex might somehow be rising from her fall. The sight was gruesome, something she knew she'd never be able to unsee. Lex was destroyed.

Movement on the lower path caught Ella's eye—Jeffrey running to the base of the waterfall.

# # #

Venn's heart pounded as he came to the waterfall. He'd been hiking down in the valley, tuned in to Ella as usual. He heard through her that the attack was happening and had sprinted up the entire way.

Any hopes of finding Lex alive disappeared the second he saw her. Her back folded at a grotesque angle over a sharp boulder. Something caught his eye, and he looked up to see Ella and Jon at the railing, starting to pull back. "Hey! You killed her!"

Venn surprised himself with the urgency of his scream. He'd heard Ella wonder how Jon had made Lex fall using only his mind. Seeing Jon with his arm around Ella and looking down on him, he wanted to rush up there and strangle them both. "You controlled her thoughts and killed her."

"No," Jon hollered back. "She attacked us and then let herself fall. I'm sorry about this, but we need to go and tell the police what happened."

They disappeared from his view.

Venn considered heading back to meet them as they came down. But seeing Lex half upside down, the water smacking off her bare stomach, he knew he couldn't leave her like that. After emptying his pockets and removing his boots, he eased himself into the icy water and half swam, half waded to the rocks, before climbing up to her.

Lex stared back at him, her face upside down, her eyes glassy, and her mouth open. There was no pulse.

Carefully and awkwardly, he strained to pick her up off the rock. He wanted to bring her back to the path and put a shirt over her face. Lex was a solid woman, and he couldn't climb high enough to get proper leverage.

He gave up and slumped on a nearby rock. Pink water streamed around his bare feet, and he followed the stream up to her long braid. As he watched the blood spiral down, he remembered how she'd braided her hair to look like Lara Croft. She'd done it for him.

She hadn't wanted to come here, he thought. She hated leaving the island of Manhattan for any reason. When he'd said it would be like a romantic getaway, she'd agreed and had been such a good sport. Venn realized that aside from her insane jealousy, she'd been exactly what he'd needed this past year. Her aggressive attitude had inspired him to do big things, including Tuning In.

Now, she was gone. His throat tightened and his jaw ached. Jeffrey Venn realized that he could cry if he let himself.

Lex was gone because Ella made her crazy, and then Gunnarson controlled her mind to make her jump. He wouldn't tell the police what had really happened, that needed to be a secret. But Gunnarson would tell him how he did it. And someday they would pay for this.

###

Jon propped up some pillows, sat on his bed, and placed the ice pack to the stitches on his forehead, dumbfounded to be ending his day in basically the same way he'd started it.

At the foot of the bed, Ella hunched over her laptop, looking up the general number of the FBI's New York field office.

They'd just finished an hour of questioning by the local police about Lex and the attack. Before that, they'd been to Thimphu General Hospital. Thankfully, Jon had come away from his fall with only a bevy of purple contusions and scrapes across the left side of his body and head.

"At least Venn didn't bring up his whole mind control theory," Jon said, referring to the police interview. "And try to pin her death on me."

"I knew he wouldn't. You're the face of Tuning In."

The murmuring of a dozen conversations came up from the restaurant and through the open window.

She straightened up. "It was rather odd though, don't you think?"

"Ella, I didn't make her kill herself."

"Oh, I know you wouldn't do it on purpose. But what if maybe you sent her a thought without meaning to? And it somehow sounded like one of her own thoughts? Like it was her own idea?"

Jon lifted the ice pack to shake his head, exhausted at the thought of having this conversation again.

"Because, if you can do that, you could make Jeffrey take down the app."

"Ella, please, no. I wasn't even thinking she should kill herself."

"What were you thinking? Do you remember?"

Jon sighed, not wanting to go back to that horrifying moment. "Well, I guess I was thinking what a frickin' monster she was. And then, of course, how I could try to stop her."

"Hmm. Maybe that first message got to her and made her give up."

They were quiet again.

Jon replayed in his mind the deeply disturbing way that Lex had held eye contact with him as she slowly fell backwards to her death. He knew it would haunt him. Plates clattered below, as though a busboy were clearing a table, snapping him out of it. "Who knows? I always felt from her this crushing blackness. Don't know how she could live with it. Maybe she just couldn't anymore."

"Yeah, I tuned in to her occasionally, mainly to figure out where she was, so I could avoid her. It was always bloody miserable. That woman truly hated herself. It's sad. But I'm still relieved she's gone." Ella went back to her laptop.

"You know," he said. "She also might've attacked us to protect Venn and the app. To keep us from stopping him."

"She always did seem like his enforcer. Either way, now we can focus on stopping the app."

The ice pack was giving him a headache, so he dropped it to the floor. "It's going to be tough," Jon said, "Considering he can tune in to us. Which he obviously does already. I mean, he must have been tuned in to know the attack was going on, right?"

"I'm sure it was me. He sends me thoughts."

"Oh yeah? Like what?"

"Hang on," Ella said. "I've found the right number."

Jon brought the hotel phone to his lap and called, then did his best to explain the situation to the FBI's operator on duty. Her patience lasted surprisingly well, until he asked for her name and location so that he could tune in to her and prove his telepathy. Just before hanging up, she informed him that making false reports to the FBI diverted attention from real emergencies and was punishable by prison sentences.

For the next hour, they emailed and left messages at the media outlets that had picked up the Tuning In story, knowing the reporters would think it was a publicity stunt but hoping that at least one would respond.

Ella eventually moved to the small desk. She demonstrated telepathy over the phone for friends in London and asked them for help. Jon continually interrupted her as he practiced sending thoughts or came looking for another kiss.

After a late dinner, he again went to her and embraced her from behind, his lips on her ear. She turned, and they kissed. He was instantly aroused. It was as though by finally letting himself care for someone, he'd become a randy teenager again.

She gently separated.

"I was only saying hi."

"We've got to focus, Jon. Maybe I should go to my cabin, so we can concentrate."

He knew she was right.

"Wait." She put her hands near her ears and looked to the floor. "He's sending me thoughts again."

"What's he saying?"

Ella held up a finger and wavered as if hit by a strong wind. She exhaled. "He wants me to go up there."

Incredibly, she seemed ready to go up, which made Jon wonder what kind of power Venn had over her, what kind of relationship they'd had. It had been enough to send Lex into a homicidal rage.

"You gonna go?"

"I don't want to. Though, I could try and get his phone and the second recording."

"Except he's tuned in to you right now and heard you think that." Jon took Ella's hands, realizing how much he wanted her to stay, how much he cared for her. "I think we should stick together. He doesn't feel any safer than Lex did."

"Okay, but I better at least send him a text." Ella rose and went out on the balcony.

Did she still have feelings for Venn? Jon wondered. He could ask her again, but he didn't want to insult her. He could tune in to her, but he didn't want to invade her privacy, either. Watching her thumbs tap away outside, he told himself to keep his eyes wide open.

Sunday, October 21

Ella dreamt of a tall monk leading an endless crowd across an open plain. The monk became Jon, and in unison, the throng fell to its knees. As though given a command.

Then Venn's voice blared like a megaphone over her dream, "Don't let him control you." She woke and jerked her head around the room, rubbing her eyes to clear the uneasy vision and message. Jon's toned body lay half-covered beside her, his flat belly rising and falling. The sheets barely concealed him. Her phone pinged and she grabbed it from the bedside table, hoping it was Jady checking in.

Nope. Another text from Jeffrey. She noted the coincidental timing. For two days, he'd been sending her jealous texts and jealous thoughts, warning her about Jon. Especially when she and Jon had been affectionate with each other.

"You fell for him right when he got new powers," the text read.

Now he was texting her at seven a.m., and she figured that the loud voice in her dream must have been him sending her a thought. Like dream spam. Great.

And what an odd dream. The monk, who'd morphed into Jon had been one of her Tiger's Nest subjects. The dream gave her an idea, a theory she had to explore.

Another text from Venn pinged: "He's controlling you."

Jon's fingers skimmed down her back and goosebumps burst across her body. "Good morning."

Ella mumbled a good morning in reply and rose, scanning the room for her bra. "We have to get something done today," she said.

He moaned as he stretched, his biceps flexing and his hair a wild tumble.

"And, having this bed right here," she said, "Makes it impossible."

Jon grinned, raising his eyebrows.

Ella couldn't help but grin with him and was an inch away from leaping back under the soft sheets when Jeffrey's latest text came to mind. "He's controlling you." Jon's gaze suddenly felt almost predatory.

She found her bra tangled in the sheets at the foot of the bed and clipped it on, Jon watching her every move. Her mind continued to veer. Had Jon heard her admiring him a moment ago? He might be spying on her right now. There was no way to tell.

"Let's promise not to tune in to each other without asking," she said.

"Okay."

That was easy, she thought, but how will I ever really know? "I'm going up to my cabin now. You're welcome to come, but no disturbing me."

"Okay."

She thought he wasn't taking her seriously. "Oliver's going to be there. You can sit in my bedroom."

"Okay."

"Because I have a theory on how to control someone else's thoughts."

They crept like fugitives up the winding wooden stairs to Ella's cabin. The hillside of tree trunks, that had first felt spacious and open, now left her feeling exposed and vulnerable. Ella wondered briefly what she was so worried about, why she was acting so afraid. Lex was gone. Then she remembered seeing Venn kick the table over at the restaurant and the way he screamed at them from the bottom of the waterfall.

They made it to her cabin without incident and she steered Jon into her bedroom to meditate. Since her dream, she'd been torn: obsessed with making the huge discovery of thought control, but also knowing it could cause tremendous harm. A modern-day Manhattan Project.

Ultimately, the thrill of discovery pushed her forward. She and Oliver worked in the main room, determining which monk was most successful at sending feelings to other monks. After an hour, she whooped. "I found him."

Oliver rolled his chair over, bringing with him a pungent cloud. Ella wondered how he could smell so bad this early in the day.

"I remember him," she said, spooked that it really was the same monk from her dream. "Monk nine, named Ugyen. He scored higher across the board in this first trial. We need to review all his recordings, find the peak scores and document the frequencies. Hopefully, there's a consistent one."

Her fingers slapped the keyboard. "Hmm, this second peak has a slightly different frequency." She pushed back from the desk and faced Oliver.

"Here's what I need you to do. First, find when monk nine's deepest matches happen, there should be thirty or forty of them across all the experiments, and jot down the frequencies for each."

"What do you mean deep matches?"

She forced a breath. "Remember we wanted to see when the monks' brainwave patterns matched each other as they sent and received messages?"

Oliver nodded.

"That's what I'm talking about," she said. "So, find them for monk nine, then calculate the weighted average frequency with deeper matches counting more. Got that?"

Oliver didn't get it. She almost snapped, not realizing her frustration came from her anxiety about her upcoming visitor. On

Friday, she'd demanded Venn's help in securing a visa and plane tickets for Jady to come to Bhutan immediately.

Ella walked Oliver through the formula, watching the time on her phone. "Once we have the right frequency, we can make a binaural track. Then I'll entrain myself to that frequency and hopefully be able to control your thoughts."

"Okay. I guess." Oliver looked as if he wasn't so sure about their project anymore.

Ella didn't have time to debate. "Great. I have to run down to the lobby. My daughter's arriving any minute." She stopped to brush her hair in the mirror by the door.

Jon came out of the bedroom, blinking. "Jady's coming here?"

Ella wondered if Jon had overheard their conversation or had been tuned in to her. "Oh hi, yes, my ex is traveling, and I couldn't go home. Jeffrey flew her here. He took care of everything."

"Awfully nice of him."

The confused, hurt look in Jon's eyes stayed with Ella all the way down the hill.

Jady burst from the van and gave Ella a tight, almost aggressive hug, the corner of her phone digging into her back. She smelled of airplanes and seemed huge, like a small woman. Her body heaved loud moans as she always did when she truly let it out.

Ella heard in her cries the relief and exhaustion from traveling alone for such a long journey. She let herself believe that Jady felt some joy in being with her mom. She decided there'd be plenty of time later to talk about the drinking episode. Ella started crying too and soon thought only of her vow to protect and reconnect with her daughter.

They declared in loud whispers how they'd missed each other, how they loved each other, and Ella couldn't help feeling a bit surprised, a bit unworthy. She tried to remember their last real hug like this and it made her cry even harder.

She felt Jady starting to let go and told herself to keep it together. She tried to hold her breath to stop herself from crying. They stepped back at the same time and Ella scanned her daughter's clothes, hair and skin. Jady wore tight jeans, the barbell was gone, and there were no tattoos in sight.

Jady grabbed Ella's forearm, bouncing on her toes.

"Guess what."

Ella loved to see her smile. She guessed that with this level of bursting excitement it could only involve a boy.

"I'm telepathic," Jady said, her eyes wide, searching for her mom's reassurance that this was a good thing.

Ella had expected moments like this on the visit, where Jady looked to her for guidance and strength, but not in the first two minutes. "What? Why didn't you tell me?"

"It happened on the airplane. I listened to your app for hours."

"Oh love, I should have warned you." She'd failed her daughter yet again. "Didn't you see my video about ramping it up?"

Jady shook her head.

"You must have been terrified."

"Kinda. You would've been so proud of me though. I remembered how Jon said to turn it off in his video."

A taxi tooted behind them, and Ella jumped. Jady's van had pulled away and they stood, oblivious, in the middle of the driveway. Ella glared at the taxi driver as if he'd almost run them over.

"Mum, over here," Jady shouldered her bag and guided Ella to the entrance. "I think it happened so fast because of those recordings you gave me."

Ella stood there speechless, happy that Jady had taken her advice over the past year to listen to the entrainment tracks but crushed with the blame for her daughter's rapid transformation.

"And everyone," Jady said. "I mean every single person in London, is talking about it. None of my friends can tune in yet. Becca thinks it's a scam. Wait till I show her."

"Everyone is talking about it? Already?"

Jady looked past her, up to the resort. "Wow, cool place."

What to say? Quick now, Ella thought. "Jady, this isn't like a magic trick. It's a big deal. We need talk about what it means and what rules we'll have, okay?"

Jady brought her eyes down to meet Ella's. She nodded with what looked like a surprised smile then looked up again.

Ella watched her, the sleeping little girl in the picture on her dresser, now approaching young adulthood. She needed her mum more than ever in a new, uncertain world, a world Ella had helped create.

Bringing her here had been the right thing to do, she decided. They'd hide out for as long as necessary, staying safe as the madness unfolded around the world. Maybe she could even figure out what was going on in people's brains.

"Jady, come with me, love. Let's swing by the front desk and get you a key."

###

Jon climbed the steep goat trail, each stride like taking three steps at once. He'd had to get out of those damn cabins and get some exercise to lose the nervous ache in his stomach. He reached the crest of the hill and collapsed against a pine tree, his lungs unable to collect enough of the thin air.

Ella hadn't mentioned her daughter's arrival today, and Jon wondered if it was because she felt guilty about Venn paying for it. What else wasn't she telling him? For the fifth time that day, he fought the urge to tune in to her. He'd made a promise.

The wind gusted, snapping him out of his mental loop.

He should be focused on stopping Venn.

As if he'd planned it, he sat with a direct view of Tiger's Nest across the valley, the tight cluster of red and white buildings seemingly stacked on top of each other. He thought of Neema, how she always had an answer and he wondered if she'd know what do about this. Yet, how could anyone possibly know about controlling someone else's thoughts?

And should he tune in without permission to a woman who spent most of her life in her mind, consulting with goddesses? Could he interrupt something like that?

On the other hand, he was trying to mitigate what might become a global disaster and every minute counted. He had no way to contact her other than hiking all the way up there and hoping that she'd be able to meet with him. Jon ultimately decided to try sending her a thought, asking if he could be in her mind and have a telepathic conversation. He knew it was rude but hoped Neema and the goddesses would understand. If she answered no, he'd hike up there and take his chances.

He went inward, focused his attention on Neema and a moment later heard from her the subtle wisdom of an ancient Buddhist manuscript she was studying. He noticed that he hadn't heard the whistling tone as he tuned in. He was also struck by the clarity of her thought and her deep understanding of the text. In the very next moment, an undefined concern rose in her, like the feeling of being watched.

She knew.

Jon fought a sense of panic, and then realized he could use that fear to create the strong urgency he needed to send her a thought. He asked her permission and she calmly answered yes, as if she'd long ago become accustomed to having someone or something else share her mind.

Jon focused on the danger Venn presented and asked for her help in controlling thoughts. It quickly became clear that he hadn't practiced enough to send sentences like Venn did, so he focused instead on concepts. Neema grasped pieces of it, and he emphasized the missing pieces until she fully understood.

She told him to wait and he heard her relay his question to another monk, who Neema knew as Ugyen. She processed his answer too fast for Jon to catch and then her mind went completely silent. There was no more discussion, no pondering his question. Not even her registering a sound or itch.

Confused, Jon tuned out and then back in to her, as if trying to reconnect a phone call or reboot a computer. The silence continued. It was like she'd left her brain. Just as suddenly, her stream of thoughts returned, as though she'd come back into a room while talking.

In formed sentences, she thought he must begin by giving up on his idea of a personal consciousness. He must completely surrender to the oneness. Let it take him, do what it would with him. Then he must focus on tuning in. Not to any particular person but to this oneness itself.

Her thoughts ran on with concepts that Jon translated into ideas he could understand. He learned he must not be afraid as he passed through. And when he arrived, he should match the state of whatever excitation in the oneness he wanted to open. Neema thought this only once and did so in a confident, matter-of-fact way. As if giving him simple driving directions.

Then she shifted her attention, too casually it seemed to Jon, to planning her upcoming trip to another monastery. He heard her think how she and almost all the monks were leaving Tiger's Nest for the night to attend a special ceremony. She considered what she should bring and whether she needed to eat before the hike. She seemed indifferent as to whether Jon remained with her or not—as though she'd already accepted his new ability.

Thunder rolled up the valley, snapping him out of his trance. He tuned out and realized that it had worked. Neema had helped him. The weight of the moment sunk in that she'd actually come back with an answer and he might have a way to control someone else's thoughts.

His excitement was short-lived. He replayed her instructions and questioned what she'd really given him: general notions of entering the collective consciousness and matching the state of an excitation. How exactly was he supposed to do these things?

From his spot at the base of the tree, Jon stared at the monastery across the valley. More heavy clouds rumbled in to block his view.

Controlling someone's thoughts was not something to take lightly. It was the kind of thing he'd need to consider from a few angles. When Jon needed to get a different perspective on something, he usually got himself upside down. And even after yesterday's attack, his favorite place to do that was at the top of the waterfall.

# # #

Jon clung his fingertips to the wet stone floor, pushing up into his handstand, trying not to fall. As always, trying not to fall made it that much harder to stay up. He eased into the pose, danced between being engaged and detached and then found stillness.

His own stillness reminded him of how still Neema's mind had been, and how she'd become perfectly silent for a few moments. He considered how, if her advice worked, he be able to control people's thoughts. Telepathy was a quantum leap in human development but controlling another person's thoughts was the stuff of gods or demons. No, he didn't have to try it if he didn't want to, he told himself. After all, he'd come to Bhutan to learn how to separate from others and this would mean connecting even deeper, going the wrong way.

But what if Ella's concern was justified? What if the app hurt or killed millions of people? Jon realized he wouldn't feel good about his decision either way and decided to keep Neema's guidance to himself for now.

"I knew it," Ella said, coming up behind him.

Jon nearly fell, taking a step with his hands to right himself.

"Sorry," she said and moved closer, as if to catch him.

Bending at the waist, he slowly brought his feet to the ground then stood.

“I heard you focusing on the sound of the waterfall and figured you were either down there or up here by our favorite hut.”

Blinking through the head rush, he registered that she’d tuned into him without asking.

“Jon, this is my daughter Jady.”

The blushing teenager shook his hand, showing braces with pink rubber bands.

“Nice to meet you,” she said.

“Nice to meet you too.”

She was a miniature version of Ella, Jon thought, with lighter hair and a few freckles. He wagged his finger between them.

“Has anyone ever told you two—”

Jady laughed. “Yeah, pretty much everyone.” She kept laughing, hand over her mouth, a case of the giggles.

Jon glanced to Ella, who seemed delighted. He thought how proudly she’d presented Jady to him. He also couldn’t help feeling this was a kind of test to see how they all interacted before continuing their relationship past Bhutan.

“What’s so funny love?” Ella said, rubbing Jady’s shoulder. She darted her eyes over to Jon.

“Oh nothing,” Jady said, taking a deep breath, “But I feel like I should bow or something. Like I’m meeting a celebrity.”

“What do you mean?” Ella said.

“His video’s at like twenty-five million views, Mum.” She looked at Jon, “A lot of people tune in to you, you know.”

He realized that he'd gone from being a hermit to a celebrity in a week. A celebrity with zero privacy. Then, with a sinking feeling, he speculated on how many people had been tuned in to him and Ella in the meditation hut the day before.

"Oh no," Ella said.

"What, Mum?"

"Nothing, love. We're just shocked to hear all this. We're a bit isolated here and we've been too busy to stay up on the news."

They shared an awkward pause.

Jady looked around. "This is a cool place."

"Yeah, but we need to go back to the cabin soon," Ella said, folding her arms as if a chill had just gone through her.

"So, what else is going on with telepathy out there?" Jon said.

"Hmm, well, I heard these people on the airplane talking about thought parties."

"Thought parties?"

"It's when a bunch of people all tune in to each other. Let's try it. Please? Just for a minute?"

"Okay, but just for a minute," Ella said.

She and Jady sat on either side of Jon on the stone bench.

"Remember, we don't have long."

"I know, I know," Jady said.

Ella turned to Jon, her face close.

"We need to talk after this," she said.

She seemed excited, but serious. The way she'd act if she wanted to talk about life after Bhutan.

"Look here, everyone." Jady held up her phone to take a selfie.

Jon's stomach tightened as he saw the three of them smiling on the screen, so close together. His stubborn subconscious misbelief was reminding him that someone like him shouldn't be getting this deep. What was he doing? Who did he think he was?

Jady took the shot and brought her phone down.

"I'm sure this is going to be a dreadful mess," Ella said, and reached across Jon's lap to take Jady's hand.

They closed their eyes.

After a moment, Jady groaned. "I hate that shrieking sound."

"Be glad it only lasts a few seconds," Ella said. "And it gets softer."

"Yeah, I don't hear it all anymore," Jon said.

They were soon squinting and shaking their heads in the overlapping, incoherent noise.

"Let's try to stay with it," Jon said. "Try to quiet our minds."

Their thoughts settled slightly, and Jon felt the love and anxieties of Ella and Jady pass through him. He shifted up to the level of knowing and heard from Ella a whirling mix of excited scientist, determined momma bear, and guilty absentee mom. Nothing about him or their relationship.

He focused on Jady and heard her feeling nauseous from the thought party but trying to stay with it since she was with Jon Gunnarson. She skipped from how nice her mother's hand felt to wanting to let go of it. Then she focused on the selfie and how her friends would react. She seemed thrilled to stand out with her new ability but also terrified to be different.

Then Jon's own mind wandered back to where it had been: his decision about Neema's latest advice.

"I feel like I'm going to be sick," Jady said, "I have to tune out."

"Me too," Ella said. "This is awful."

Nausea welled up Jon's throat and he too tuned out.

"Why would anyone want to do that?" Ella said.

"No idea," Jady said. "But I'm never doing it again."

"It's too bad," Jon said. "I'd thought that tuning in to a bunch of people could be a way to block other people from hearing me. That it would sound like noise to whoever tried to tune in to me."

"It's noise all right, but you can't do it for more than a minute," Ella said.

"And you can't really hear yourself think either," Jady said.

Ella stood and faced Jon, her face bright. "I may have the answer."

"Answer to what?" Jady said.

Jon rose, knowing immediately what she meant.

"And I want to hear what Neema told you," Ella said.

Jon thought again how she'd been tuned in to him in his handstand, breaking her own rule. And how she was going to pressure him to try controlling Venn's thoughts.

On the stone path back to her cabin, he decided that once he and Ella were alone, he'd remind her about asking permission to tune in. And since he was flying home tomorrow, they should talk about life after Bhutan. Even though, at that moment, he wasn't totally sure what he wanted.

# # #

Venn clicked a button and Max Harding's bloated face filled his screen.

"Yes, I heard you," Harding said. "Yes, it's fucking amazing. This whole thing is fucking amazing. You're changing the world."

"I know," Venn said, his right leg bouncing. "We're looking at a billion-dollar business."

"Not when they seize Person8 and put you in prison."

"That's why I'm sending thoughts to them."

"Oh, please. That's ridiculous. It's not gonna work. It sounded like some creepy voice in my head when you did it to me. I knew it wasn't me. Unless these guys think you're God telling them to leave Jeffrey Venn alone, they're not gonna stop."

"I know, I know. Ella's working on making it sound like their own thoughts. I could basically control them."

"That would be, uh, incredible. She better figure it out fast."

"I've been listening to her. Right before this call she said she had the answer. I gotta tune back in to her."

"Wait, what day is it there? Don't you fly out tomorrow?"

"Yeah. If I fly out."

Harding cocked his head. "If you don't show for the magistrate, you're toast. You want your picture on that Most Wanted page? Right next to some fucking terrorist?"

"Max, I gotta go."

Venn ended the call and got back into Ella's head.

# # #

Ella tore off her headphones. "It's not working, is it?"

Jon took off his headphones as well. "No. Felt kinda slow."

"Damn it," she said. "I thought monk nine would at least get us closer to directing thoughts."

She'd based her new track on the average frequency of when one of her monks had most deeply matched the other monks, hoping it would put her into a deep enough state to control thoughts.

Jon said, "Scientific method, keep trying, right?"

Ella thought he seemed almost pleased. She wondered why that would be and was tempted to tune in to him to find out. But she also but had a nagging feeling that Oliver may have made a mistake.

"Before I give up on this, I'm going to double-check Oliver's work. He's not the sharpest tool in the shed."

She shooed Jon to the bedroom to sit and she began the laborious process of spot-checking Oliver's work. Ten minutes in, she hadn't found any errors, and the more she thought about it, the dumber her theory seemed anyway.

The front door opened, and Oliver rushed in, his eyes wide.

Enough of this shared office space concept, she thought. It was time to get a new card key.

"Oh, hey, what's going on?" he said, out of breath from running up the stairs, but still trying to act nonchalant.

"Double checking our work. It looks okay though."

Oliver came to the desk and looked past her, to her screen, as though he'd known she was digging through his files.

How could he have known? Ella wondered.

"Oliver, are you telepathic?"

"No. No, not at all. I only get bleeding headaches from that track."

Ella turned back to her screen, to close her eyes and tune in to him. His thoughts faded in—jumpy and uneasy with unasked questions about what she'd seen, whether she knew. Whether she knew what, Ella asked herself. "No really, you can tell me," she said. "Can you tune in?"

As Oliver denied it again, she heard in his mind concern about why she was prodding him and whether she knew about the recording. Ella felt like she'd been hit in the gut and had to ask. "Did you give Jeffrey the last track, the track of Jon while he sent me a thought?"

His eyes gave him away, but hearing his thoughts left no room for doubt.

He opened and then closed his mouth.

She heard it dawn on him that his thoughts were being heard at that very moment. That lying was futile.

Looking to the floor, he nodded. "I'm sorry, Ella."

Ella searched the desk for any of his personal items and heard Oliver worry about how Venn would react to his being found out. Jeffrey, she realized, must have alerted Oliver that she was going through his files, which meant he was monitoring her. It made her stomach tighten again.

She handed him a maroon Cheney School pen and a blue and green planet earth stress ball, one in each hand, like a formal ceremony. "Give me the card key to my cabin."

He did, his face even paler than usual, his thoughts swirling on whether she'd tell his father.

She definitely would.

"Get out. And stay away from me and my daughter."

Oliver looked up, ready to beg her not to tell his father, but he must have seen in her hard stare there was nothing he could say. With an audible sigh, he turned and then shuffled out the door.

The rat, Ella thought, and tuned out of him. Although, how could she expect him to stand up to someone like Jeffrey Venn? After all, she wasn't going to confront Jeffrey on this. She just had to hope he didn't put that thought-sending track on the market.

She had to direct his thoughts, but her flimsy theory hadn't panned out. The very idea of directing someone else's thoughts seemed more far-fetched than ever. So, what now? she asked herself. Well, first she had to pee.

She tiptoed past Jon and Jady and into her bathroom. After using the toilet, her phone pinged with a text from Venn, as if he'd been waiting for her to finish, which was yet another level of telepathy creepiness.

"Sorry your theory didn't work," his text read. "Don't give up! :)"

###

Venn tuned out of Ella and stood, glaring at the ceramic Buddha statue on his side table. After a moment, he came to his senses, picked up the statue, and hurled it against the wall, where it exploded, raining sharp pieces across the hardwood floor.

He'd been tuned in to her for most of the day, enduring hours of her painfully boring work and pathetic insecurity with her daughter. Then, when it finally came time to test her stupid theory, nothing. To top it off, she'd fired Oliver, his man on the inside.

He went to his last bottle of K5 Himalayan Whiskey and splashed the counter as he filled a glass. At least she'd kept Gunnarson's hands off her today, he consoled himself.

The whiskey tasted like liquid, smoky hay.

Gunnarson had to be controlling her mind, he thought. Otherwise, how could she give up Jeffrey Venn to be with that spooky freak? How could she give up something that for once felt real?

He took another sip and remembered hearing Ella having sex with Gunnarson in the meditation hut the day before. How he couldn't resist being hugely turned on for every devastating second. Then of course Lex's attack and fall. He knocked back the rest of his glass, wincing with the burn.

Lex, he knew, had been a ticking time bomb. In fact, the more he thought about it, the more likely it seemed that she'd just killed herself. Hell, she'd tried twice before. Maybe there was no thought control.

A dizziness came over him and he steadied himself on the counter. This wasn't where he wanted his thoughts to go, he told himself. It was just the liquor going to his head.

Deep into his second, daylong stakeout of Ella, he realized he hadn't eaten, shaved, or showered since… well, he couldn't remember. And while for once he didn't care how he looked or smelled, he knew had to get some food in his system.

Lurching out of his cabin and along the winding path, he imagined what Ella might be doing. Hopefully, not banging Gunnarson again. Maybe having Jady here would keep them in check.

He paused at the top of the steps, realizing that she hadn't eaten all day either. He was about to tune back in to her, to send her the thought to eat, when he straightened and picked his head up. No, he told himself, he could stay tuned out of her for more than five damn minutes. He wasn't obsessed. He only tuned in to her to learn how to control thoughts, so he could stop the FBI.

Once he got some food, he'd have the energy to start again.

###

Jon heard Ella come out of the bathroom and sit next to him on the bed.

She whispered in his ear. "Come tell me what happened with your nun."

Damn, she remembered, Jon thought.

They came to stand in the middle of the main room.

"It was pretty strange actually," Jon said. "We had this conversation in our minds. But it was just more of her riddles."

Ella raised her eyebrows, ready to solve anything.

"First," he said, "You tuned in to me without asking, remember? When you found me by the waterfall?"

"I know, I'm sorry. You weren't answering my texts and I wanted you to meet Jady."

"Well, let's stick with our deal, okay?"

Ella nodded and came to hold him.

Their first fight, if you could call it that, Jon thought. It had come out alright and it felt so nice, so *right* to hold her.

"It's also because I'm a bit freaked out," she said. "Just trying to keep it together, you know?"

"Oh, I know," he said. He'd meant to commiserate but when she stayed silent, he realized he might have sounded like he was teasing her. After all, he did literally know exactly how she was feeling.

She sighed and pulled back to look at him. "I mean, everything's new, and happening so fast. Tuning in helps me know I can trust you. I think we should tune in more, so we don't misunderstand each other."

Jon thought she might be right; he often wished he was tuned in to her. Then his old fear kicked in and his gut clenched, just as it had when Jady took the selfie.

"We can talk too, you know," he said.

"True." Ella stepped back. "So, please, tell me everything that happened with Neema."

Jon drew a breath. "It took a while for me to learn how to communicate, but once she understood, she asked another monk for advice, I think his name was Ugyen, and then she disappeared."

"Wait. Ugyen?" She squeezed his hand, hard. "He's monk nine. What did he say?"

"I couldn't make it out but when Neema came back from being brain silent, she was very clear." Jon described how Neema told him to become ego-less and not be afraid. How he should tune in to the oneness. How he should enter into the other person and match their state.

Ella arched her back and stretched her shoulders as she took it all in. She caught him admiring her and smiled. “Focus, Jon.”

“You’re naturally distracting.”

“I guess to tune in to the oneness, you just set your intention. What did she mean by entering the other person and matching them?”

“Like I said, she speaks in riddles.”

She pursed her lips in thought. “It seems like for sending thoughts, you need a specific frequency and you happened to find it. Maybe to insert a thought which sounds normal to the other person, it’s not about finding a certain frequency. What if it’s about matching *their* neural network frequencies? Emulating the other person’s brainwaves?”

“Thinking exactly like they do. A lot easier said than done.”

She took his hand again. “Maybe not for you. You’ve been hypersensitive to other people’s frequencies your whole life. And you said you could control your whistling tone, right?”

“Yeah, but we don’t even know what that was.”

Ella bobbed her head, as if she couldn’t believe she was even having this conversation. “Well, what if you were controlling your brainwaves? Setting your frequency at will.”

Jon took his hand away. Her pep talk made it seem almost possible he could do it, which made him even more uncomfortable.

“Let’s try,” Ella said, her eyes radiant with renewed hope.

Jon had no choice but to nod.

She pulled two low chairs together.

He sat and gazed out the huge windows. For some reason, Venn's warning to Ella came back to him, "watch out for his mind control." Jon considered if he'd ever, in a more subtle way, controlled or influenced other people's thoughts without realizing it. It was impossible to know for sure. In a few seconds, his mind sped like a server farm through forty years of interactions until hitting his last eye gazing session with Danielle. Why had she been so wildly attracted to him?

Jon failed in controlling Ella's thoughts, repeatedly. Eventually, he tuned out and simply looked at her, holding her warm, now sweaty hands. He reflected on how he'd seen her in the video a day before learning of the Tuning In opportunity. How it had been this woman, not the thousands of other people he'd met in his life, who'd triggered his transformation. He realized he was failing because he wouldn't let himself do it. He couldn't mess this up.

"I trust you, Jon. Trust yourself," Ella said out loud.

He felt Ella's excitement and got the sense that for her this was about discovery, another new scientific frontier she'd be a part of exploring.

"Yes, of course I want to make history again," she said. "But we also need to stop Jeffrey, stop that app, until we know what it's doing to people's brains. Look, if you don't trust yourself, trust me, because I'll be tuned in to you and will hear what you're doing every step of the way."

Jon puzzled how that would work, how he could control her thoughts if she knew what he was doing. It didn't make sense. He nodded and quickly switched to focus on her mala bead necklace, hoping she'd missed his fleeting realization.

He felt like he could handle some of Neema's guidance—to become egoless, fearless, and surrender. He supposed that when the time came he'd figure out how to tune in to the oneness and then match the state of an excitation. Whatever an excitation was.

Slipping easily into a transcendent state, he imagined himself a drop of water mixed into the ocean. He set his intention on tuning in to the oneness, tuning in to *everything*. After a time, the high-pitched whistling returned and grew to become deafening, like he was inside a jet engine. A searing whiteness filled his mind's eye, like he was staring into a spotlight. This was the infinite white wall he'd seen in his mind's eye many times before. But never so 'close'. He'd always known it was some kind of boundary but he'd always stopped. He reminded himself not to be afraid this time. After all, why fear the sound if he couldn't go deaf, the light if he wouldn't go blind?

Soon it felt as though every molecule in his body were vibrating, like a complete sensory overload, as if he were ready to explode. He remembered Neema's advice to surrender and let it take him.

Barely perceptible at first, the discomfort began to ease. The whistling and vibrations were morphing into a symphony of harmonic tones that seemed to run through him. Black triangles at the edges of his mind's eye slowly expanded, turning the wall of light into a massive, blinding white circle.

The circle came into focus, and he gazed in awe at a swirling bundle of pure energy, bright as a star, intricate as a human eye. Its translucent center refracted like a diamond, and out of it, glowing silver petals bloomed continuously. They spiraled outward in a fractal, naturally occurring geometry. He stared, mesmerized and found that depending upon which pattern he focused on, the petals spun clockwise or counterclockwise around the core.

This wasn't a dream or hallucination. This was crisp, high-definition reality. Jon somehow knew this thing related to him but instead of trying to label it as his spirit, mind, or consciousness, he thought of it as a sun, his sun.

As the petals bloomed to the edge, they dissolved into a mesh of countless fibers, pulsing with colorful light and swaying like sea grass. His sun was melding into the surrounding field, as if it were simultaneously dissolving into and being created out of it.

And this field all around him had a fluid texture of its own. Ultra-fine, transparent fibers flowed in overlapping waves in all directions, their colors correlating with the pitch of the harmonic tones he heard.

It continued to slowly recede and he felt like an astronaut watching his ship float away. How could he separate from his own sun, he wondered? From himself? But he had no sense of panic. More than anything, he felt infused with love.

He also felt weightless, with no physical sensation at all. Not his hands resting on his lap, his feet on the floor or even his breathing. How strange not to breathe, he reflected. Like an endless moment of deep stillness between breaths. A formless consciousness.

His point of view rotated, like a slow, precise back flip that lowered his swirling sun out of sight, and he realized this had happened just as he'd begun to wonder what else was around him. He'd moved as the specific idea was arriving, perhaps just before.

Two more large suns swung into view as he turned, one closer than the other. And beyond, smaller points of light were scattered about, some clustered together and some lonely pinpricks of light in the distance. A surreal but oddly familiar universe. Like a sea of suns.

In fact, he realized he'd known this place his whole life. Even before his life. All the way back to the Big Bang. That it was the only thing that was real. He thought how this must be the oneness, the field of consciousness, and these suns must be the excitations Neema spoke of.

He somehow knew the larger sun was Ella's and the one behind it, Jady's. They were similar to his own, with blooming, swirling petals, but Ella's center was golden, her petals were a mix of purples and blues. Breathtaking.

He remembered Neema's guidance to *match the state*, and immediately he passed into the core of Ella's sun. He came into an infinite room, a kaleidoscope of vibrant purples, blues, and gold. Taking in the surrounding psychedelic sky, he also noticed that Ella's thoughts had grown louder, somehow blending with high frequency tones and colors here. Still, he found he could think independently. Traces of orange and red appeared in the swirling sky and with them a came a heaviness, a pressure bearing down on him. He tracked a particular streak of orange, arcing like a comet, and in the next instant he was following it, hurtling, tumbling through the endless sky of color.

He heard a steady tone and let it in as if he were deep under water and opening his mouth to breathe. He brought from his own mind the specific thought for Ella, "Check on Jady."

The comet shifted to blue and then shot out of her core and away from her sun, Jon riding it all the way out. It dissolved into the field and radiated away, and Jon turned back to Ella's sun, indulging in the soothing, glowing mandala for what might have been a minute before deciding to return to his own sun, not sure at all whether he'd accomplished what he'd set out to do.

It took less than a second, a painless blur, for him to move away from Ella's sun and to reenter his own. He fluttered his eyes open, disoriented and dizzy for a moment to be back in his physical body.

Ella was coming back into the main room, closing her bedroom door behind her. "Sorry," she said. "I didn't hear anything from you. It was like you disappeared. So I thought I'd check on how Jady was doing."

###

Jon felt Ella's fear rise.

She opened her eyes wide. "Really?"

"Really," Jon said. "That's what I thought for you to do."

The color drained from her face. She slid down the doorframe to sit on the floor. There was no pacing and no exclamations about making history this time.

He went to sit next to her.

"Thanks. I'm okay," she said. "I guess I never thought we'd actually figure it out, you know?"

For a long moment they sat on the hardwood floor, holding each other in silence.

"We can't tell anyone about this," Ella said.

Jon kept himself from reminding her that anyone tuned in to them at that moment already knew.

"Sometime," she said, "I want to hear about what you went through, but right now we have to stop the app."

"Okay. I'll try to direct him now."

"No, wait. We need to make sure it's working. I need to watch him while you're doing it. Let me see where he is."

Ella tuned in to Venn. "He's eating, seems like he's down at Beyul. Let's go to your cabin and maybe I can watch him from the balcony. I'll leave a note for Jady in case she wakes up."

They hurried down the hill, the sun low and buried behind thick clouds.

"I'll have him do something simple first," Jon said. "Like rub his face. So we can be sure it's working."

"We don't have time, Jon. He'll find out about this." Ella checked her phone. "I haven't gotten a text from him yet, which means he's probably taking a break from spying on me. We got lucky. I say you just go for it, get him to stop the app right now."

Jon tried to imagine all the steps that Venn would have to take to make that happen.

"Hopefully I can give him a high-level idea, like, take Tuning In off the market, and it'll stick with him."

"Yeah. I don't know. Let's see how it goes, I guess."

Once inside his cabin, they headed straight to the balcony.

"You were right," he said, peering down to the terrace.

"He looks dreadful," she said.

He is dreadful, Jon wanted to say. "Looks like he's finishing up his dinner."

"And like he's going for hike afterward."

Venn wore his boots and hiking belt, the knife hanging below his seat.

"Okay, I'm going in," Jon said. "It may take a while. How long did it take with you?"

"Not long. Like twenty seconds," she said.

"Really? It felt a lot longer to me. Time must move slower in the field."

"What?" Ella shook her head. "Never mind." She jerked her thumb toward the bedroom, *stop stalling*.

Before going back inside, he held her face and kissed her as if he were leaving on an epic journey. Which of course he was. Then he sat on the corner of the bed, closed his eyes and even though he was prepared for it, the experience of slowly pulling out of his physical body still rocked him to the core. When he came into the ethereal, alternate universe, he saw what looked like a mini constellation of suns. He recognized Ella's and just as he wondered how he'd find Venn's, he swooped in front of a glowing red and gray sun and *knew* it was his.

It also continuously bloomed from the center but instead of rounded petals, Venn's had cones. And only a narrow tunnel from the outside to the orange and red core. The tones Jon heard and felt now were a low, machine-like hum.

He glided closer, feeling the pressure rise around him as though descending in deep water. He told himself he could do this; he could go to Venn's level.

Suddenly, the cones became swirling spikes and the tunnel to the core closed off. One of the spikes extended and lashed out, knocking him with a precise blow.

He tumbled away, back past his own and Ella's suns. He thought to return and instantly zipped back to Venn, this time to find dozens of sharp-looking tentacles violently whirling like a three-dimensional saw. He took his time, watching for openings and planning his attacks but failed on three more tries.

After what felt like ten minutes, he sailed past his sun for the third time. His sun looked different. He stopped abruptly. His sun looked as if it had begun shrinking and blending back into the field. Even more odd, he had the sense he was viewing it simultaneously from all sides. Something was definitely different.

Not good, he thought. He went back into his body and woke lying on his bed, choking for air and coughing up water. Water was up his nose and in his lungs. It hurt.

"Why are you doing this to me?" Venn said, holding Ella by the shoulders and trying to get her to look him in the eye.

Jon wiped his nose and mouth, took a careful breath and made it to his feet.

"Ella, what happened here?" he said, pointing to his soaked shirt.

Venn's hands fell away, and she came to him.

"I'm so sorry. You weren't responding."

"So, you tried to drown me?"

"I couldn't wake you, Jon."

Venn touched her shoulder again and said her name, more hurt than angry.

Her phone pinged in her pocket. She looked to her screen as if to avoid looking at Venn. "Jady needs me."

She glanced to Jon, her expression asking if it was okay for her to leave. Jon nodded, and she rushed out of the cabin, seeming more relieved than anxious.

Venn turned to Jon for the first time, as though just noticing him in the room. His blotchy face and baggy, bloodshot eyes matched the stress and despair Jon felt coming from him.

"Tell me how to do it," Venn said. "I'm paying you, remember." He gave a weak smile and slumped into the desk chair. "Come on, talk me through it."

"I'm not teaching you anything."

"Hey, everyone's going to figure it out eventually." Venn slurred his words slightly. "You might as well."

Jon shook his head and felt Venn's frantic desperation rise.

"Do you think telepathy's a good thing?" Venn said, drilling his eyes into Jon's. "I mean, will it be good for society?"

Jon considered how many outrageous coincidences had lined up to make the new Tuning In app a reality. If felt as if telepathy were meant to be.

"I do."

"Well, if I'm arrested, they'll shut down my company and stop the app before it has a chance." He brought his palms together in front of his chest. "I've done some things I'm not proud of, but we can't let that kill what we've made together."

Jon tore his gaze away and the image of Venn's spiky red sun returned to his mind. "You need to take this app off the market until we know it's safe."

He felt Venn's rage rising, ready to burst. Jon tried to let it in and let it pass through him. He didn't think he could control Venn's thoughts, and he knew he'd never talk him into stopping the app. Hopefully, the FBI would catch up with him.

Jon rose and left without another word. Halfway up the hill, he heard a long, tormented howl from inside his cabin.

Ella let Jon into her cabin and stopped him just inside her door. "You okay?"

"Yeah. Venn's losing it though. We've got to stay away from him."

"Why didn't you control him?"

"I couldn't, he closed up. He must have been tuned in to you and figured out what I was doing. Who knows? Maybe people can block being controlled if they know what's going on."

"That's not good. Damn."

"Mum, can we go now?" Jady called from the bedroom.

Ella pushed out a breath. "Jon, we have to talk about this but she's hungry and so am I actually. Join us for dinner?"

"Of course," Jon said. He wouldn't have left them alone anyway.

"Let's go up to the bar. I can't eat another meal in here, and I heard Jeffrey go back down to Beyul for another drink."

It was Sunday evening, so the resort was mostly empty, and they had the Nalu Bar to themselves. They sat in comfortable chairs around a low wooden table. A fire pit roared next to them.

The waitress took their order and disappeared down the hill to the kitchen, where she'd likely stay until their food was ready to haul up.

To make sure Venn wouldn't surprise them, Jon sat facing the stairs, tuned in to Venn's endless, angry mental monologue.

Jady peppered him with questions. Did he have any kids? Was he married? Where was he going after Bhutan?

He kept his answers brief. Sadly, there wasn't much to say, plus he sensed that Ella wanted to catch up with Jady. The question of where he was going next stuck with him as he watched them talk. He tried to imagine himself building a normal relationship with Ella and reminded himself to talk with her after dinner.

"I think we should tour the country a bit," Ella said to Jady. "You can miss some school considering everything that's going on."

Jady nodded while she yawned. "I can't wait to sleep in tomorrow." She brought her arms around herself. "It's so windy. Can't we eat in the cabin?"

"Sorry, I cannot eat one more meal in that room," Ella said.

Jady gave Jon a pleading look, snapping him out of one of Venn's more vindictive mental rants. "Oh. How about I run down and get some jackets?" He took Ella's card key and hurried down to her cabin, determined to find the jackets and return quickly. Once inside the still room, alone for the first time since entering the field, he paused. Venn was nursing his whiskey and didn't seem an immediate threat, so he tuned out for a much-needed moment of peace. The sheer strangeness of everything caught up with him.

He'd found another side of reality, like another dimension, which seemed to him like the foundational underpinning of the visible world. Now, in the silent room, he noticed that what he'd experienced in the field still lingered at the edge of his awareness, like a dream that continued after he'd woken up. He needed time to sort things out but with Venn like this, now wasn't the time.

The thought of Venn sent him searching for jackets and then bounding back up the steep stairs. Two short, wiry waitresses carrying trays of food, blocked his way, and he imagined Venn yelling in Ella's face at the table. When he arrived with the waitresses, Ella and Jady seemed relieved at his return. Or it might have been the food.

After they'd devoured spicy beef stew and rice, Jon leaned back and watched mother and daughter tease each other about how much they'd eaten. He again noticed how the world seemed different, as if he had a deeper, transparent kind of awareness.

The waitress clearing the plates, the elderly bartender dozing behind the bar, and even Ella and Jady laughing, all felt to Jon as if they were only acting. The tables around them, the yellow and orange Bhutanese flag flapping at the edge of the patio, the surrounding trees, swaying in the wind, all seemed to have no physical essence, no substance.

There was definitely something happening there on the hilltop, he thought. And while he was seeing every detail with his eyes, it felt more like he was watching a movie, or a hologram. Like none of it was real.

But he was okay with that. Because he also felt a powerful and very real interdependence with everything around him; a deep sense of oneness that transcended thought. As if all his personal boundaries had fully dissolved, and even the edges of his physical body had softened.

"Earth to Jon," Ella said.

He sat up.

"What's he up to?" she said, asking about Venn.

Jon kicked himself. It had been so nice to have only his thoughts that he'd gotten carried away. "Sorry, hold on."

He tuned in to Venn, ready for more anxious muttering about his flight to New York the next morning. What he heard and felt instead was a simmering rage at Ella and him, blaming them for his downfall and scheming ways to get them to teach him thought control by paying, begging, ordering, or threatening. He heard Venn convince himself that threatening them was the only way. He finished his whiskey and began psyching himself up, thinking that he'd have to mean it, since they were probably spying on him. If they wouldn't help him, he'd hurt them until they did. They deserved it.

Jon tensed, realizing that for Venn, what had started as a means to an end had become an end in itself. He knew Venn wanted vengeance for losing Ella, for losing Lex, for losing his company and his incredible discovery.

He heard Venn take out his long hunting knife and test its sharpness. Jon instinctively looked to the table and around the patio for weapons: a dinner knife, a chair, a log. Nothing seemed good enough.

He wouldn't consider bringing Ella, Jady, or the bartender into a knife fight, and help was a long way off; he hadn't seen any resort security all week. No, staying up here meant he'd be fighting Venn alone and unarmed.

"We have to go," he said, rising. "Now."

Ella and Jady looked up, eyes wide.

"He's coming up. He wants to hurt us."

They stood, their metal chairs scraping on the stone patio.

"If we hurry, we can make it to your cabin," he said.

"He has a card key."

"If we go to my cabin, we'll run straight into him."

"Can't you, you know, stop him?" Ella said, chopping her hand through the air.

Jon had disarmed opponents holding wooden props but never the real thing. The last two times he'd practiced aikido, he'd been slammed to the ground. He shook his head.

"Then what?" Ella said.

The voice gave Jon the answer. The same voice he'd heard in his fight with Neema. He looked across the valley and a calmness came over him. "We need to run. Follow me."

He led them into the dark woods, heading up the ridge, his mind embracing the childlike logic of a big heavy door, a place they could hide. The logic that had literally been spoken in his mind.

"Where are we going?" Ella said, already out of breath.

"I know a place to hide by the stream."

"What? That's your plan? Hide in the woods?"

Jon shook his head and pointed up to the monastery, feeling foolish for trying to trick Venn with misdirection.

"But, Mummy," Jady yelled. "What are we doing? Why are we running?"

Ella explained their situation in between breaths.

The sky was darkening by the minute, and gusts of wind carried small drops of rain through the trees and onto their faces. Jon reassured himself that Venn would probably get lost, may even tumble off that cliff. This line of thinking only made him doubt whether the three of them might do the same. He remembered Neema saying to let the voice be his guide and had the fleeting, silly hope that it might keep him on course like a navigation app.

After a few minutes, Jady said she couldn't run anymore, and they slowed to a fast walk.

Venn now sounded even more unhinged, more dangerous, as though the pursuit and hearing Ella's fear were fueling his fury. He began to think in clearly formed, threatening sentences, "I know where you are. You can't hide from me. I'll hurt you and Jady if you don't teach me to control thoughts."

Jon fought to keep his focus, to remember the correct pattern of ridges to follow, and he almost walked right past the trail. "This is it, we found it," he said.

Once on the trail, more in the open, the rain pelted them in large, heavy drops.

"This is a hell of a hike," Ella said. "In a storm? At night?"

"We cut off half the climb. We'll be safe there."

"Why don't you just direct his thoughts, tell him to leave us alone?"

Venn thought in sentences now. "I'll block you again. And you didn't stop Lex either. She killed herself. I'm not afraid of you. I'm coming after you and you can't stop me."

"He might be right," Jon said to Ella. "I may not be able to stop him. And while I'm trying, he'll catch up to us."

Thunder boomed, and the skies opened, washing them in a heavy, cold rain.

Jady slipped on the muddy path and fell, crying out.

"Jon, this is madness," Ella said.

Blinking water from his eyes and helping Jady up, he recognized how ridiculous his plan would seem to her. And how silly it might really be. He also knew this wasn't the best time to explain that he'd been guided by a voice that Neema had said could be the body of reality itself. "I know, but if I can actually control other people's thoughts," Jon spoke loudly over the rain, almost shouting. "He can't learn how to do it, or he'll control us. Control you. Get the FBI to back off. And who knows what after that? Think what a guy like him would do with that kind of power."

Ella shook her head diagonally, half yes, half no.

"I can do this, Mum," Jady said, shivering next to her mother. She wore a waterproof jacket but had changed from her jeans into short shorts, and her thin legs glowed white in the dark. For the next hour, Ella held her hand and practically pulled her up the trail, past the waterfall and up the final flight of seven hundred stone steps, equal to the height of an eighty-story building.

Panting, the three of them shambled to the front entrance. The door was locked.

Jon banged and then kicked and then yelled.

The white monastery loomed over them, the high windows watching.

He'd heard from Neema that the monks were gone for the night but still, Jon thought, wouldn't at least a few of them have stayed behind? He knew that the dormitories were on the far side of the compound and realized that at this hour, and with the heavy rain, they'd never hear him down there.

No one came.

He'd led Ella and Jady on a two-hour trek to a locked fortress. A dead end. He visualized a fight with Venn and his knife.

Ella gripped his forearm, and he turned to see her staring blankly, her hair matted to her face, no doubt hearing Venn thinking something terrible.

He had to keep them away from Venn. He had to find way in. The front door was solid and so was the lock. The windows were twenty feet off the ground and the wall was sheer and slippery.

Jon left Ella and Jady on the stone porch, shivering and leaning against the door, and moved to the left edge of the building. As he remembered, it fused into a sheer, vertical cliff, which towered over him for hundreds of feet. He tried different hand and foot holds, hoping to make it to the roof, hoping that he'd find a door or window to enter up above.

Water was streaming down the cliff, and six feet off the ground, his foot slipped, and he fell, hitting the stone patio hard on his side. He stepped back, saw how high he'd need to climb, how far he'd fall, and decided to try the other side.

Walking to the right edge of the building, he knew he'd find another sheer, vertical cliff, this one dropping two thousand feet down to the valley floor. A white metal fence, chest high, separated him from a narrow ledge on the far side. Moving slowly so not to slip, he scaled the fence. Once on the ledge, gripping the fence, he leaned out to peer around the corner of the building.

The heavy wind hit him immediately with a blast of rain in his face. Squinting, he saw by the faint light from an upper monastery window that the ledge he stood on continued along the cliffside wall and angled up gradually to an overhanging eave where it narrowed to about three feet wide.

Still clutching the fence, he snuck a glance down behind him. Silver sheets fell into blackness. As though he were standing on the rim of a black hole. It was more terrifying than if he'd seen the full cliff. He turned back, trying to push the image from his mind and then looked to the entrance, ready to be swayed by a smiling thumbs-up or a head shaking *no way*, but he could only make out Jady's pale legs poking out from the doorway.

His sense at the Nalu bar that the world was an illusion had disappeared. What to do? Where was the voice now? Why would it have brought him here if he couldn't even get in without killing himself?

He imagined Venn appearing at the top step and the two of them grappling with the knife. He knew how badly it could end and knew he had to try the ledge. And he'd have to be fast.

Focusing on slick stone under his sneakers, he crept around the corner and inched along the wall. In the faint gloom of the distant light, white paint splatters glowed along the ledge. The steady wind suddenly eased, and he nearly lost his balance. His hands swept the rough, wet surface, searching for handholds. He leaned into the wall, moaning with each breath. In his panic, the wall felt as if it were pushing him backward and his mind played the scenario of him losing his balance, tumbling over the sheer drop, and disappearing into the void. He focused on his breath and the moment passed.

Venn was coming, he told himself, He had to get inside. He started moving again, each step a carefully tested decision and soon felt the ledge rising. He ducked under the eave and then twisted and pulled himself up onto the slick roof of the entrance building, raindrops banging all around him on the painted metal.

At the far end of the roof, he climbed over a wooden railing onto a small balcony and, to his immense relief, found the door unlocked. He knew Venn might be tuned in to him but at this point he didn't care. Let him try this insanity too.

The room was pitch black except for a thin line of light at the base of the far wall. After three steps, his toe caught a meditation pillow and he fell. The old wooden floor made a faint cracking sound under his weight. He fumbled his way to the door and then came out into a lit hall with walls and floors of tightly fitting stone.

Suddenly anxious whether he'd made it in time, he rushed down the stairway and then across the entrance hall to the main door. He turned the iron latch, swung open the door and Ella and Jady fell backwards onto his shins. He helped them up and then put Jady, still half asleep, on his back.

Ella closed and locked the door behind them with a satisfyingly loud boom.

The monastery wasn't warm, but it was a huge improvement over the wind and rain.

He led them up the stairs, calling for help. His voice echoed through the dark chambers. They reached the first temple and found the large open room empty and silent. Their wet clothes dripped on the polished wide-beam floor. He started to call again but bit it off, asking himself what he wanted of these monks anyway. What did he expect? For them to fight for him? To convince Venn to go away? To call the police?

He had no right to be there. Not only were they trespassing on one of the world's most holy sites, but now he wanted to drag these peaceful people into a conflict? No, he needed to avoid the monks and hide until morning. Venn would surely head back to the resort in a few hours to catch his flight. If he didn't, the monks would return tomorrow and by sheer numbers force him to leave.

Jon, Ella, and Jady shuffled through the first temple. And then up the long, straight stone steps to the cave temple. And then into the dark, empty chamber where he'd met with Neema. In pitch-blackness, they crept to the low table and cave door on the far side of the room. Jon patted his hands around the table, looking for matches to light the candles. He touched the coil of string and tiny blade Neema had used to make his bracelet and then found the jar of wooden matches.

The candlelight improved their moods dramatically. Jady flopped onto a large cushion and huddled over the tiny flames as if it was a campfire.

Moments later, Jon shivered outside at the top of the temple steps. It was the best place, he'd decided, to confront Venn if he made it this far. The doors had no windows, so he had to stand outside, listening to Venn's mind and watching the doors in the courtyard below.

The voice had told him to go into the cave but, now that he'd mulled over every scenario, the idea didn't make sense. Venn would hear where they were, and they'd be cornered.

He'd needed to fight him off. He reminded himself to tune out of Venn as soon as he saw him so that he didn't repeat his defeat with the karate fighters. He visualized how the fight would go; Venn coming up, knife out, Jon waiting until he made his first lunge and then twisting the blade from of his hand and bringing him down on the flat entryway. It was no more than a wide step, he noticed. There was not a lot of room for a scuffle, and the stone stairway was steep and long.

You could die falling down that.

He'd been listening to Venn's thoughts for half an hour and still couldn't tell exactly where he was. Venn did a good job of not thinking about his surroundings. He kept repeating his threat to hurt them unless they taught him how to control thoughts.

The door behind him opened slowly. He moved to the top step for Ella to squeeze out.

"Hey. Aren't you freezing out here?"

"Yeah, but this is the best place to stop him."

Ella looked down the stairs and nodded.

"How's Jady doing?"

"Still cold but sleeping again."

Thunder shook the valley, deep and low.

"I think we'll hear him when he's trying to get in here, don't you?" Ella said. "He'll be thinking about it."

"I hope so."

"I had an idea. How about I stay here on lookout, and you try to direct his thoughts again? Get him to go back to the resort. If I hear him getting close, I'll wake you up."

"Okay, I'll see if I can, but he probably already knows what I'm doing." Jon opened the door. "Please don't drown me this time."

"You're totally unresponsive. It's like you're dead."

"Okay, well, I'll try to come out more often." Jon went inside and sat on a cushion on the far side of the table, his back to the cave door and facing the front of the room. Ella's words stayed with him. He had a fleeting image of himself dying here, then pushed it out of his mind.

Jady was breathing heavily on her pillow at the end of the table, fast asleep.

He looked around the gloomy room, imagining Neema sitting in this spot for countless hours. Maybe she could help him again. He tuned in to her and heard her repeating a mantra of the Tibetan words, "om mani peme hung." He also knew from Neema that she was asking for the attention and blessings of Chenrezig, the embodiment of compassion. Jon regretted interrupting her, but this qualified as a matter of life and death. He sent her thoughts asking for help and telling her of the danger he faced.

The mantra continued unabated.

Discouraged, he tuned out of her and left his body.

# # #

Ella stood in an exhausted trance. She watched the rain as she listened to Venn's thoughts. He was making a rational case for them to teach him, but underneath it she heard his bitterness, his desperation, his sense of betrayal. She understood.

She heard his frustration about the locked front door to the monastery. Rushing inside, her wet sneakers slapped the smooth cement floor. The candlelit scene in front of the cave door was like something out of a horror movie. Jady lay sprawled on her back, mouth open, across a large cushion. Jon sat motionless and unresponsive.

Based on her experience trying to wake him, Ella knew she needed to splash him and choke him with water. She looked around for any kind of bowl or cup and was mad at herself that with Venn's thoughts continuously running through her head, she hadn't better prepared herself for this moment. She pulled one of the thick red candles out of its copper cup and rushed outside to fill it up.

The big drops flowing off the eave seemed to splash as much water out of the cup as filled it. She heard Venn inching along the ledge as Jon had. Finally, with what might be enough, she hurried back inside and emptied it square in Jon's face.

Like a statue, he made no reaction.

She dashed back out to refill the candleholder and heard Venn climbing onto the first temple roof. After an agonizing minute and her heart pounding, it filled, and she ran back to Jon, almost falling on the slippery floor.

This time, she lowered him carefully onto his back next to Jady, amazed at how heavy he was. As she brought him down, his weight pulled her off balance and she fell on top of him. He seemed like a corpse, his skin cold and pale.

She opened his mouth and splashed the water into his nose and mouth. He remained motionless for a moment, in a deep coma, and she worried he wouldn't wake, that she'd drowned him.

She heard the rain grow louder for a moment, as if the door had opened, but when she turned to look, saw only darkness.

"Wake up, Jon. Wake up dammit."

# # #

Jon woke choking, a searing pain in his lungs. He convulsed and turned on his side to cough up water, thinking that there had to be a better way to bring him back.

Jady screamed.

He lifted a hand, his eyes watering, to tell her he was okay, but she wasn't looking at him. He followed her gaze to see Venn, dripping wet, his chest heaving, on the other side of the table.

How in the hell did this happen?

Venn's hands were empty, the knife in its sheath at his hip. Jon felt the anger and desperation blasting from him like a furnace.

Ella and Jady were already standing, and Jon scrambled to his feet, the four of them around the small table and the candles lighting their faces from below.

Venn looked to Jon. "Why didn't you stop me? Can you even do it?"

Jon felt buffeted by Venn's anger. The rain hummed on the metal roof.

"I blocked you?" Venn said, having heard either Jon or Ella answer his question in their mind.

"That's right," Jon said.

"Probably because I know what you're up to. You did control Ella though; I heard her thinking about it. I'm sure it wasn't the first time he controlled your thoughts. Teach me how. Make me a new recording. Whatever we need to do. And I'll pull the app off the market until it's been tested."

Jon doubted he'd keep his word. And he couldn't let Venn control people's thoughts, especially Ella's. "You need to leave now."

In one swift movement, Venn pulled out his knife and grabbed Jady's arm.

She screamed as Venn jerked her away, into the dark. "Stay back," he said.

"Jeffrey, stop," Ella said. "I'll tell you everything, right now." In a shaky voice, Ella explained Neema's guidance.

"That sounds impossible," Venn said.

"You can try it, right now," she said.

"I saw Gunnarson lying in a coma there. I'm not doing that around any of you."

"Jeffrey, I told you everything we know. Please let her go."

"I need to make sure I can do it. He needs to teach me."

Jon's eyes flicked down to the table and back.

Venn looked to the table as well. "Use that cord. Tie them to that column," he told Jon, "And then go into the cave."

Jon started to shake his head.

Venn put the blade to Jady's neck. "Do it. Don't test me."

Fumbling in the gloom, Jon tied Ella and Jady's hands together around narrow a stone column.

Venn put the knife to Ella's throat and ordered Jon into the cave.

Jon slid back the three large iron bolts, the metal squeaking, and swung the heavy door open. A gust of frigid air came over him as if he'd opened a vast, dark refrigerator. In the dim light, he saw it stretching back, deep into the mountain. The front part felt a small room. He stepped inside, and the door slid shut behind him with a tight thud, surrounding him in pitch-blackness. The locks slid with muffled squeaks and bangs.

"I'll kill you if you hurt them," Jon said to the door.

Pure silence and pure darkness surrounded him. Almost as otherworldly as the field.

Guru Rinpoche's legendary cave, he thought. Where the voice had wanted him. Stunned how he'd ended up here, he replayed the scene outside and remembered flicking his eyes down to the table. It was as if he'd tried to show Venn the cord, as if he'd tried to get himself locked away. Was this, he wondered, how it felt to have your thoughts controlled?

He tuned in to Venn and the noise of the other man's thoughts layered on top of his own. He heard Venn trying to calm his mind, to go inward and do what Ella had told him.

As Jon waited, a simple question appeared in his mind, fully formed, as though it had been patiently waiting for this very moment. Had he really controlled Ella's thoughts this afternoon? or had the idea to check in on Jady been Ella's? Given the situation, it's what any mother might have done. Had his amazing thought control actually been a coincidence? He heard Venn think of things for Ella to do, like stand on her toes and shake her head. After a few moments, his angry voice came through the door.

"How do I know she's not cheating? that she's not tuned in to me?"

Jon searched the blackness for an answer to that riddle. "Did you leave your body? Go into a coma like I did?"

"No. It's not working. Tell me how to do this, or she gets a new scar on her face."

If Jon hadn't really controlled Ella's mind earlier, he couldn't help anyone else do it. But he knew Venn wouldn't believe him. Jon imagined Venn in a rage, hurting Ella. He flung himself at the door, banging and screaming to be let out. In between his screams, he heard a shriek from outside and stopped, leaning on the cold wood, his heart leaping in his chest.

"You don't understand, Gunnarson." Venn spoke quietly, inches away on the other side of the door. "I'm either a billionaire or a convict. I'll do whatever it takes."

Jon knew he meant it. "I'm not sure how much you'll see, but I'll try to show you. Tune in to me."

Venn agreed, and Jon slid down the door to sit on the cold, wet rock. He closed his eyes and instantly felt as if he were floating in space. The full sensory overload began as his consciousness left his body, but this time it felt natural, beautiful even.

He came into the field and spun to see Venn's spiraling gray and red sun. He felt Venn's impatience and knew he had to work quickly to get into his sun and stop him.

Jon spotted small pulses of light that came from deep inside the spiraling orb and moved up a spiky tentacle right before it lashed out. Maybe, he thought, he could predict and avoid the movements.

He moved closer, saw a pulse, and dodged one tentacle only to be hit by another, hurtling him away.

When he returned, dozens of tentacles spun and whipped in a frenzy, their movements almost too fast to see. Jon couldn't imagine how he'd get through that violent defense. And if he did, would he be able to come back out? Would his consciousness be trapped inside Venn's?

He should go back to his body and fight Venn to the death, he decided. But he'd stuck himself in this cave. At a loss, Jon lingered in place. He soon noticed he was moving, as if buffeted by currents. Waves of colorful energy flowed in all directions, gently rocking and swaying him.

Neema had said his movements came out of the space around him. He realized that thinking and planning hadn't worked in his last two aikido fights or here in the field. So he let go completely, becoming one with the field.

A powerful current picked him up into a lightning-fast orbit around Venn's sun. He found himself swooping and avoiding every strike. The action was far too fast and complex to follow but the timing and direction of his movements was perfect. As if he were in the zone during an aikido fight. He darted between strands and then arrived before Venn's core. A spiraling red orb.

That was not me, he told himself. And this time, he was okay with it.

The heaviness he'd felt before now felt crushing. Still, he moved inside the core, into a shrieking, grayish-red inferno. Venn's thoughts dominated, and Jon knew his impatience, suspicion, and rage at not being able to hear Jon's thoughts.

Venn was thinking that Jon must not care enough about Ella. Venn thought he needed to go into the cave and hurt Jon to get his way. The threat was real. Jon imagined his body, lifeless and vulnerable, and fought the temptation to give up. He knew he only had a few moments. He tried matching Venn's frequency, but simply couldn't get low enough.

The strange voice returned, overriding everything. "Om mani peme hung."

What Neema had been chanting, Jon thought. He repeated the words and better understood what made Venn the way he was. He needed Jon's help, not to control thoughts but to overcome his deep-seated fear, to keep him from hurting anyone.

Jon focused on making himself ready and available to help. All at once his own frequency dropped, to a level he hadn't felt since his mother's death, and he matched Venn's frequency.

He brought to mind the thoughts he wanted Venn to think. That he should accept his situation and untie Ella and Jady. That he'd learned all he could here, and it was time to leave.

As Jon repeated these thoughts, he swirled around the core faster and faster. The colors around him started to shift from red to orange.

After a time, Jon's perspective shifted, to a kind of omniscience, as it had when he'd seen his sun blending into the field earlier that day. As it had when his body had been dying.

He flashed out of Venn's heavy sun and came in front of, above, and around a spinning diamond, emitting a faint high frequency whistling. It was his home frequency, but with no blooming petals, just his core, dissolving back into the field and fading.

He shot into his diamond and then opened his eyes, to candlelight and pain.

Monday, October 22

Jon soared through a bright blue sky. Like an angel. Or a ghost. The wind caught in his ears, and the sun warmed his back.

On the ground below, countless statues covered a vast desert, each a variation of the serene Buddha that sat on his porch in California. They crowded to the horizon, sitting upright, eyes shut, hands resting in their laps. Their stone faces tracked him in silence and then, as one, millions of stone eyes opened and stared.

At that same moment, as if the two events were connected, a ceremonial gong clanged outside the window of the Tigers Nest dormitory. Jon jolted awake, confused where he was. Sturdy wooden bunk beds filled the cold, shadowy room, lined in perfect rows. The previous night came back to him. Venn had untied Ella and left the monastery, and when she'd opened the cave door, Jon had slid back and banged to the stone floor.

He rubbed the back of his aching head and thought how odd that the voice had maneuvered him into the cave. As though putting him into a position where he'd have no choice but to give himself completely to the field and use only compassion to prevail. He replayed the ethereal voice in his mind, trying to find any clue on who or what it was. Maybe Neema was right, maybe it was the body of reality, the field, communicating with him. Why not?

Neema would return here soon, he realized. He had so much to tell her. He also wanted to apologize to Ella and Jady for how he'd handled the situation with Venn. The voice may have helped him grow but it would have been far easier on them if he'd tried to physically subdue Venn at the resort.

He pushed himself up from the horsehair mattress. Every part of his body hurt. The past few days had been rough: karate fighters breaking his nose, Lex tasering him over the railing, and the stone floor nearly cracking his skull. He pulled on his cold jeans and shuffled to the hall.

He found them huddled together in the kitchen. They shared a maroon blanket around their shoulders and warmed their hands by a potbelly stove. He came closer, silent in his socks.

Ella was speaking to Jady in a gentle tone. "I promise, love. I'll always be here for you. As much as you'll let me."

Jady nodded, her head on her mother's shoulder.

Jon wanted to hug them both. "Good morning."

"There you are." Ella turned and frowned. "Are you alright?"

"Cold and achy. But yeah, I think so. How about you two?"

"Starving," Jady said.

"A nice old monk told us pilgrims will be here soon, offering rice porridge," Ella said. "As yummy as that sounds, we'd like to head back to the resort for some eggs and bacon."

"Then a day at the spa," Jady said, throwing off the blanket and stretching.

Jon thought of how they might run into Venn and started to object.

Ella beat him to it. "I tuned in to Jeffrey earlier and he's on the run. Driving through what seemed like northern India."

"Really? Okay, well, sounds good," Jon said, abandoning his plan to wait for Neema.

Jady cheered. Then she announced she needed to pee and trotted off to the bathroom.

Ella came to Jon and took his hand. "When I was tuned in to Jeffrey earlier, he must have guessed I'd be tuned in to him. He thought stuff for me. He told me he was listening to me. That he'll always be with me."

Jon nodded. At some point, he wanted to hear the full story of their relationship. "Try to forget about him. How about I check on him from now on?"

Ella hugged him, her body warm and strong. "That would be great."

Back at the resort, under a hot shower, Jon replayed parts of his conversation with Ella on their hike down from the monastery. He'd asked her plans for the day—one of those questions that mean much more—and she'd only mentioned showering and checking her email.

Jon wasn't too concerned. With Jady just arriving yesterday, he knew they'd stay for at least a few more days, which would give him plenty of time to figure out if he and Ella had a future beyond Bhutan.

He dressed in his least dirty t-shirt and khakis and bounded down the zigzag stairs to Beyul. The restaurant bustled with a crop of new guests. Many of them turned as he entered, as if they'd been expecting him.

Ella and Jady sat at a round table for four by the window, heads bent to their devices. As Jon moved through the dining room, Oliver rose from a nearby table and held up his phone to take a video.

Within seconds of sitting down, Jon's chest tightened to the point that he found it hard to breathe. He reminded himself to allow it in and let it run its course. "Is everything okay?"

"No, everything's not okay," Ella said. "Everything's a disaster. I thought people would look past the app and see what a groundbreaking discovery this is, but no, I'm getting hammered by my boss, my peers, even my father. And of course the press all say I should have known better, that *I'm* the one to blame here."

The unsaid end to her sentence, "not you and Venn," hung in the air. The waitress arrived and Jon had to focus to place his order given Ella's consternation and the excitement of the entire room humming through him.

Once the waitress had left, Jady spoke to her screen. "You really should see what's going on, Jon."

He took out his phone, but before diving into the headlines, he snuck a glance at the two women, fixated by their screens. He felt an odd mix of belonging and aloneness and thought how the other guests might see the three of them as an average American family. He also noticed that the tightness in his chest was easing, as if by him not resisting, Ella's stress was passing through him. Maybe he didn't need to disconnect after all.

When he woke his phone, the photos app appeared. He swiped past the recent selfie of him, Ella, and Jady in front of Tiger's Nest and saw the picture of Ella in the YouTube video. He passed her his phone. "See the date here? I took this almost three weeks ago. The day before I even heard about Tuning In."

She put her hand to her mouth. "Look how short my hair is. And that's Simon Morris. He's still at University College London."

"Let me see, Mum."

She handed Jady the phone, then squinted to Jon. "That's very strange, isn't it? In more ways than one. Do you make a habit of this sort of thing?"

Jon laughed. "No, you're the only one."

"Wish you'd stayed at UCL," Jady said.

The table went quiet again. Cutlery clinked on plates around them.

Jon took back his phone. He opened the browser and found that the Tuning In app dominated the headlines, with pictures of Jon, Ella, and Venn in every story. The most popular one of Jon had him striking a yoga pose on Lex's deck, shirtless and with a noticeable bulge in his shorts. Cringeworthy.

"Number one app on Apple and Android," Jady said. "An estimated five thousand people are already telepathic."

"No way," Jon said. "Really?"

"I'm not surprised," Ella said. "Jeffrey targeted people who were already using entrainment apps, so they transformed quickly. That number will spike up in a few months when the average users catch up."

Jon found an article in *The Guardian* that focused on his and Ella's budding romance. It read like a tabloid. He decided not to mention it.

"Mum, listen," Jady said. She read from her phone. "Based on reports from telepaths tuned in to Ella Sandström, Jeffrey Venn appears to be in northern India, on the run from the FBI."

Ella gave a deep sigh. "It's bloody awful," she said. "Knowing that people, complete strangers, are listening to your thoughts nonstop."

The table went quiet again, no one sure where to look or what to say.

"We have to ignore it," Jon said. "Hopefully it'll calm down after a while."

"Oh, you think so?" Ella said. "Have you seen your Twitter feeds yet?"

"My what? I'm not on Twitter."

"You are now," Jady said. "Hold on a sec." she tapped her screen a few times. "Here, have a look."

It took him a few moments to figure out what he was seeing. A new tweet posted: "JG HIMSELF is reading @JonsMind for first time right now! Hello #JonGunnarson." Jon scrolled down to previous tweets: "JG catching up on headlines. Shocked by telepathy growth." "JG breakfast with ES and JT. Feels anxiety from ES about her career." It took a second for Jon to realize that JT stood for Jady Talbot because Jady went by her father's last name. An earlier tweet troubled him the most. "JG anxious about what's next for him and ES. Hoping to stay together after Bhutan."

Ella read out loud from her screen. "@JonsMind is a Twitter feed run by three telepaths who stay tuned in to Gunnarson and report his primary thoughts and actions in real time. The feed already has four hundred and sixty-two thousand followers."

In a clear inner monologue, he cursed the telepath spying on him. He gave Jady her phone back and wondered why anyone would care what he was doing minute by minute.

"You're famous Jon," Ella said. "I mean, we all are but after those videos, I think people see you as a prophet. Some kind of a God even."

He stared blindly at his glass of water. A week ago, he'd arrived here a lonely, desperate man. Now he was a God?

"I know," Ella said. "It's insane. But like you said, we have to try and ignore it. Live our lives."

He resisted the urge to see whether his curse had been tweeted. His breakfast of eggs, peppers and spicy rice arrived. As he took his first delicious bite, he couldn't help but imagine how it would be described by @JonsMind.

"Politicians in the States are calling for the app to be banned," Jady said.

"Yeah, I can imagine why," Jon said. "No more lies, right? I think telepathy could do the world a lot of good."

"It might, but it also might not matter as much as you think," Ella said. "A lot of people will still only believe what they want to believe. But the app should be illegal until we know it's safe."

Jon thought how it was too late, how the spread of telepathy might be slowed, but that copies of his recording would forever be out there.

"Mum, I'm done. Can I go to the spa now?"

"I don't know, Jady," Ella said. "I need to see what flights we can get on later today."

"Today?" Jady's mouth hung open.

"Yes, love. Sorry, I have to be back at Oxford as soon as possible."

"I got here yesterday!" Jady rose from the table. "I thought—" She threw down her napkin and rushed out of the restaurant.

Ella sat back, watched her go.

Jon felt the heavy, crushing rush of sadness and guilt from her and reminded himself not to resist and to allow the feelings in.

"I feel awful putting her back on a plane, I really do. I want to be a better mother to her. But come on, I'm at the middle of all this, the biggest scientific discovery of our lifetime."

Jon noticed Oliver holding up his phone again, shamelessly taking a video.

"I have to answer to a lot of people," Ella said. "I have to get to the bottom of what's happening in our brains. I feel personally responsible."

She stood, and Jon did as well, his mind racing. He realized there wouldn't be any long, quiet days here to pick the perfect time to talk. He had to say something now.

He took her hand. Conversations paused around the restaurant, and more than a few patrons turned their heads.

"I understand," he said.

"I hope so, Jon."

"We haven't talked about us yet."

Ella's eyes widened. "Do we need to? I mean, I know how you feel about me, and you must know how I feel about you."

"Well, I guess," he said. "I haven't been tuned in to you much."

"Then tune in to me more. How's this, I love you, Jon Gunnarson."

His chest swelled as if he'd taken a huge breath. "I love you too, Ella Sandström." He pulled her close, her clean hair soft on his face, her body fitting his perfectly.

The room full of diners burst into applause and cheers, startling Jon and Ella. Beaming faces surrounded them, like a wedding reception, and they soon found themselves shaking hands and posing for pictures. The restaurant manager insisted on buying their meal and eventually, with his help, they made it out to the lobby.

"Oh my God," Ella said. "That was something."

"Yeah, I feel like a movie star."

"I guess we really are famous. Will take some getting used to." They held each other's gaze and the aviary fell quiet, as if even the birds were listening in. "I should go to Jady. And yes, you should come with us to London."

Jon smiled. He'd just been thinking the very same thing.

END OF BOOK ONE

THE SEA OF SUNS

Jon, Ella, and Venn are back together in Book Two of the series. Millions are now telepathic, and Jon finds himself the leader of a global movement. All he really wants is to hold on to his new life with Ella. But when she discovers that a new drug which blocks telepathy threatens the world, they must find a way to stop it. The question is, how can they stand up to Venn and his new powerful friends who will kill to get what they want?

AUTHOR'S NOTE

Thank you for reading TUNING IN. Reviews are the lifeblood of authors. So, if you enjoyed this book, please give it a positive review wherever you bought it.

And book two of the series, THE SEA OF SUNS, is available now. Please look for it wherever you buy your books :)

Learn more at www.richardhroberts.com

ACKNOWLEDGMENTS

I'm grateful for the guidance of my two amazing editors: Victoria Mixon for helping me overhaul my original story and challenging me to base how telepathy might be possible in scientific truth, and Elizabeth Kracht for helping me present the complex character Jon Gunnarson and believing in me as a writer. And thank you David Drummond for your creativity (and patience) in creating a truly unique cover design.

My sincere thanks to the brilliant scientists, aikido sensei and empaths who generously gave their expertise and inspiration to this project:

- Mary Lee Esty, PhD, Founder of the Brain Wellness and Biofeedback Center of Washington DC
- Frank Echenhofer, PhD, Professor of Clinical Psychology and Neuroscience at the California Institute of Integral Studies in San Francisco, CA
- Dean Radin, PhD, Chief Scientist at the Institute of Noetic Sciences in Petaluma, CA
- Richard Strozzi-Heckler Sensei, Aikido Shichidan (seventh degree black belt), Head Instructor and Founder of Two Rock Dojo in Petaluma, CA
- Chetan Prakash, PhD in Mathematical Physics, independent researcher on mathematical theories of consciousness, Aikido Rokudan (sixth degree black belt), and Head Instructor of Redlands Aikikai in Redlands, CA
- Jamie Ginsberg, Founder of Marin Power Yoga in San Anselmo, CA
- Rev Scott Smith, DD, SSC, Empath, Healer and Founder of Shaktify.com
- Penney Peirce, Clairvoyant Empath and author of Frequency

I'd also like to thank the friends and family who were subjected to multiple drafts of this novel: Tiffany, Maureen, Jonathan, Tiffany,

Robert, John, Melissa, Andrew, Armineh, Michael, Paul, David, Duncan, Wendy, William, Jean, Huw, Lily, and Charlie.

Made in the USA
Monee, IL
29 August 2022